"Becky's hardly a beauty, is she?"

The Baron laughed softly. "You know I like Becky, mama. She's a good nurse and she's been through a rough patch. Shall we say she's not quite my type. I'm not attracted to thin mice."

It was a pity that Becky heard him as she came into the room. The self-confidence she had so painfully built up since she'd been with the Baroness oozed out of her sensible shoes.

Boiling with rage and humiliation, she almost missed what the Baron was saying. "We're going to Molde for a few days and we'd like you to come with us."

The arrogance of the man! Throwing her a holiday like someone carelessly tossing a bone to a dog. Nothing, Becky vowed fiercely, would make her go with him.

OTHER
Harlequin Romances
by BETTY NEELS

Many of these titles are available at your local bookseller.

For a free catalogue listing all available Harlequin Romances, send your name and address to:

HARLEQUIN READER SERVICE,
M.P.O. Box 707, Niagara Falls, N.Y. 14302
Canadian address: Stratford, Ontario, Canada N5A 6W2

The Promise of Happiness

by

BETTY NEELS

Harlequin Books

TORONTO·LONDON·NEW YORK·AMSTERDAM
SYDNEY·HAMBURG·PARIS·STOCKHOLM

Original hardcover edition published in 1979
by Mills & Boon Limited

ISBN 0-373-02301-4

Harlequin edition published December 1979

CHAPTER ONE

THE road over the moors was lonely, its surface glistening from the drizzle which had been falling since first light. It was still very early; barely six o'clock, but already full daylight by reason of the time of year—the end of June, but as yet there was no sign of the clouds breaking, so that the magnificence of the scenery was a little marred by their uniform greyness. There were no houses in sight and no cars, only a solitary figure marching briskly on the crown of the road, the thin figure of a girl, wrapped in a shabby old-fashioned raincoat, her hair tied in a sopping scarf. Marching beside her was a black retriever, no longer young, attached to a stout string, and tucked under the other arm was a plastic bag from the top of which protruded a cat's head. It was an ugly beast, made more so by its wetness and a battle-scarred ear, but it was quiet enough, taking no notice of the road but fixing its eyes on the girl's face.

'We're free, my dears,' she told them in a rather breathy voice, because she was walking so quickly. 'At least, if we can get to Newcastle we are. The main road's only another mile; there may be a bus,' she added, more to reassure herself than the animals.

'Anyway, they won't find we're gone for another two hours.'

The dog whimpered gently and she slowed her steps, and said: 'Sorry, Bertie.' Without the animals she could have got away much faster, but the thought hadn't even entered her head. They had been her solace for two years or more and she wasn't going to abandon them. She began to whistle; they were together and hopeful of the future; she had a pitifully small sum in her purse, the clothes she stood up in, by now very wet, and a comb in her pocket—there had been no time for more; but she was free, and so were Bertie and Pooch. She whistled a little louder.

She intended to join the A696 north of Newcastle with the prospect of at least another six miles to go before she reached the city. She had been walking through moorland, magnificent country forming a small corner of the National Park, but very shortly it would be the main road and Newcastle at the end of it.

The main road, when she joined it presently, was surprisingly free from traffic and she supposed it was too early for a bus. She began to wonder what she would do when she got there and her courage faltered a little at the prospect of finding somewhere to spend the night, and most important, a job. And that shouldn't be too difficult, she told herself bracingly; she was a trained nurse, surely there was a hospital who would employ her and let her live in—which left Bertie and Pooch ... And they would want references ... She was so deep in thought that she didn't hear the big car slowing behind her and then stopping a few paces ahead. It was a large car, a silver-grey

Rolls-Royce Corniche, and the man who got out of the driving seat was large too and very tall, with pepper and salt hair and very blue eyes in a handsome face. He waited until the trio had drawn abreast of him before he spoke. He said 'good morning' with casual politeness and looked amused. 'Perhaps I can give you a lift?' he offered, still casual, and waited quietly for his answer.

'Well, thank you—but Bertie and Pooch are wet, they'd spoil your lovely car.' She looked it over before her eyes went back to his face.

For answer he opened the back door. 'There's a rug—your dog can sit on it.' He studied Pooch's damp fur. 'Perhaps the cat beside him, or would you rather have him on your knee?'

'Oh, with me, if you don't mind, it's all a bit strange for him.'

He opened the door for her and when they were all settled she said contritely: 'We're all so wet—I'm sorry.'

'It's of no importance. Where can I set you down?' He smiled fleetingly. 'My name's Raukema van den Eck—Tiele Raukema van den Eck.'

'Rebecca Saunders.' She offered a wet hand and he shook it, still with an air of amusement. She really was a nondescript little thing, no make-up and far too thin—her pansy brown eyes looked huge and there were hollows in her cheeks, and her hair was so wet he could hardly tell its colour.

'Where would you like to go?' he asked again, and this time there was faint impatience in his voice.

'Well, anywhere in Newcastle, thank you,' she made haste to assure him. 'I must look for a job.'

'A little early in the day for that, surely?' he queried idly. 'You must have left home early—you live close by?'

'I left home just before four o'clock. It's six miles away, down a side road.'

Her companion shot her a quick glance. He said on a laugh: 'You sound as though you're running away from a wicked stepmother!'

'Well, I am,' said Rebecca matter-of-factly. 'At least, she's not exactly wicked, but I had to run away; Basil was going to drown Pooch and shoot Bertie, you see.'

'I am a very discreet man,' offered Mr Raukema van den Eck, 'if you would care to tell me about it ...?'

Her hands tightened on Pooch's fur so that he muttered at her. 'I can't bother you with something that's—that's ...'

'None of my business? I have always found that talking to a stranger is so much easier—you see, they are not involved.'

'Well, it would be nice to talk about it ...'

'Then talk, Miss ... no, Rebecca.'

'People call me Becky, only my stepmother and Basil call me Rebecca.'

He had slowed the car as the country round them was slowly swallowed by the outskirts of the city, and his 'Well?' was encouraging if a little impatient.

'I'm twenty-three,' began Becky, 'my mother died when I was eighteen and I looked after Father at first and when I went to Leeds to train we got a housekeeper. Everything was lovely ...' she swallowed a grief which had never quite faded. 'My father

married again. He died two years ago and my stepmother forced me to go home because she said she
was ill and needed me . . .'

'People don't force anyone in these days,' remarked her companion.

'Oh, yes, they do.' She wanted to argue with him
about that, but there wasn't much more time. 'She
wrote to the Principal Nursing Officer and her doctor
wrote too. She sent Basil—he's my stepbrother, to
fetch me. She wasn't really ill—jaundice, but not
severe, but somehow I couldn't get away. I tried once
or twice, but each time she told me what she would
do to Pooch and Bertie if I went, and I had no
money.' She added vehemently: 'I don't suppose you
know what it's like not to have any money? It took
me almost two years to save up enough money to get
away.'

'How much did you save?' he asked idly.

'Thirty pounds and sixty pence.'

'That won't go far.' His voice was gentle.

'Well, I thought for a start it would pay our bus
fares and breakfast before we look for a job.'

'Will your stepmother not look for you?'

'Probably, but they don't get up until eight o'clock.
I call them every morning—they'd wonder where I'd
got to. But by the time they've asked the housekeeper
and looked for me that will be at least another hour.'

'And what kind of job do you hope to get?'

'Well, nursing, of course, though I suppose I could
be a housekeeper . . .'

'References?' he probed.

'Oh—if I gave them the hospital at Leeds my stepmother might enquire there and find out—there isn't

anyone else, only my father's elder brother, and he lives in Cornwall, and I don't expect he even remembers me.' She turned to look at him. 'I suppose you couldn't ...?'

'No, I couldn't.' His tone was very decisive.

She watched the almost empty street and didn't look at him. 'No, of course not—I'm sorry. And thank you for giving us a lift. If you'd stop anywhere here, we'll get out.'

He pulled into the kerb. 'I am a little pressed for time and I am tired, but I have no intention of leaving you here at this hour of the morning. I intend to have breakfast and I shall be delighted if you will join me.'

He didn't sound in the least delighted, but Becky was hungry. She asked hesitantly: 'What about Pooch and Bertie?'

'I feel sure we shall be able to find someone who will feed them.'

'I'm very obliged to you,' said Becky, any qualms melting before the prospects of a good meal.

He drove on again without speaking, threading his way into and across the central motorway, to take the road to Tynemouth and stop outside the Imperial Hotel.

'Not here?' asked Becky anxiously.

'Yes, here.' He got out and opened her door and then invited Bertie to get out too, handing her the string wordlessly before entering the hotel. He was looking impatient again and as she hastened to keep close, reflecting that the hotel looked rather splendid and that probably the porter would take one look at her and refuse to allow her in—especially with the animals.

She need not have worried. Her wet raincoat was taken from her and leaving Pooch and Bertie with Mr Raukema van den Eck she retired to the powder room with her comb to do the best she could with her appearance. And not very successfully, judging by her host's expression when she joined him.

They were shown into the coffee room where a table had been got ready for them and what was more, two plates of food set on the floor beside it. Becky took her seat wonderingly. 'I say,' she wanted to know, 'do all hotels do this? I didn't know—breakfast at seven o'clock in the morning and no one minding about the animals.'

Her companion looked up from his menu. 'I don't think I should try it on your own,' he suggested dryly. 'They happen to be expecting me here.' He added: 'What would you like to eat?'

Becky hesitated. True, he drove a Rolls-Royce and this was a very super hotel, but the car could go with the job and he might have intended to treat himself to a good meal. She frowned; it seemed a funny time of day to be going anywhere ...

'I'm very hungry,' said Mr Raukema van den Eck. 'I shall have—let me see—grapefruit, eggs and bacon and sausages, toast and marmalade. And tea—I prefer tea to coffee.'

'I'd like the same,' said Becky, and when it came, ate the lot. The good food brought a little colour into her pale thin face and her companion, glancing at her, looked again. A plain girl, but not quite as plain as he had at first supposed. When they had finished she made haste to thank him and assure him that she would be on her way. 'We're very grateful,' she told him, and Bertie and Pooch, sitting quietly at her feet, stared up in speechless agreement. 'It's made a wonderful start to the day. I'll get my coat ... would you mind waiting with them while I go? I'll be very quick ... you're in a hurry, aren't you?'

'Not at the moment. Take all the time you need.' He had taken a notebook from a pocket and was leafing through it.

Becky inspected her person in the privacy of the powder room and sighed. Her hair had dried more or less; it hung straight and fine down her back, a hideous mouse in her own opinion. She looked better now she had had a meal, but she had no make-up and her hands were rough and red and the nails worn down with housework. She didn't see the beauty of her eyes or the creaminess of her skin or the silky brows. She turned away after a minute or two and with her raincoat over her arm went back to the coffee room. She was crossing the foyer when the door opened and three people came in; a large, florid woman in a too tight suit who looked furious, and a small, elderly lady, exquisitely dressed, looking even more furious, and seated in a wheelchair pushed by a harassed-looking man.

'I am in great pain,' declared the little lady, 'and you, who call yourself a nurse, do nothing about it! I am in your clutches for the next few weeks and I do not like it; I wish you to go.'

The large woman put down the wraps she was carrying. 'Foreigners,' she observed nastily. 'They're all alike. I'm going!'

She took herself off under Becky's astonished stare followed by a gleeful chuckle from the little lady, who said something to the man behind the chair so that he went out of the door too. It was then that her eye lighted upon Becky. 'Come here, young woman,' she ordered imperiously. 'I am in great pain and that silly woman who calls herself a nurse took no notice. You have a sensible face; lift me up and look beneath my leg, if you please.'

Becky was an obliging girl; she twitched back the rug covering the lady's knees in preparation for lifting her and saw why she was in a chair in the first place. One leg was in plaster, the other one had a crêpe bandage round the knee. 'Which leg?' asked Becky.

'The bandaged one.'

It was a pin which shouldn't have been there in the first place, its point imbedded behind the lady's knee. Becky made soothing noises, whisked it out, pocketed it and tucked the bandage end in neatly. 'That must have hurt,' she said sympathetically. 'Can I help with anything else?'

The little lady smiled. 'No, my dear, thank you. You've been kind.' The man had come back with a small case under his arm. 'I'll go straight to my room and they can send up breakfast.' She waved goodbye and Becky heard her telling the porter to let her know ... she didn't hear any more as the lift doors shut.

She went back to the coffee room and was a little surprised to find that her host seemed in no hurry at all. All the same, she bade him goodbye and marched resolutely to the door. It was still raining outside and she had no idea where to go, but she refused his rather perfunctory invitation to stay where she was for an hour or so; he must be longing to be rid of them by now. She went off down the street, walking as though she knew just where she was going, although she hadn't a clue.

Mr Raukema van den Eck stood where he was, watching her small upright person out of sight. If he hadn't had an appointment he might have gone after her ... it was like putting a stray kitten back on the street after letting it sit by the fire and eat its fill ... He frowned with annoyance because he was becoming sentimental and he didn't hold with that, and the waiter who had just come on duty hesitated before sidling up to him.

'The Baroness is here, Baron,' he murmured deferentially.

'Just arrived?' He glanced at the man. 'She's in her room? I'll come up at once.'

He ignored the lift, taking the stairs two at a time, to tap on the door which had been indicated to him. It was a large, comfortably furnished room and his mother was sitting, still in her wheelchair, by the window.

'Mama, how delightfully punctual, and was it very inconvenient for you?'

She lifted her face for his kiss and smiled at him. 'No, my dear—Lucy was charming about it when I explained and William took the greatest care of me, and after all we didn't have to leave until six o'clock.'

Her son looked round the room. 'And the nurse?'

His mother's very blue eyes flashed. 'I have given her the sack. A horrible woman; I knew I should not like her when she arrived last night, the thought of spending three weeks in her company made me feel ill, and only a short while ago, as we arrived, I begged her to help me because of the pain and she would not. So I sent her away.'

Her son blinked rapidly, his mind running ahead. Here was a situation to be dealt with and he was due to leave in less than an hour. 'Where was the pain?' he asked gently.

'It was a pin, in the bandage round my knee—at the back where I could not get at it. There was a girl in the foyer—a skinny little creature with enormous eyes; she knew what to do at once when I asked for help. Now why cannot I have someone like her instead of that wretched woman they sent from the agency?'

The faint but well-concealed impatience on the Baron's features was replaced by a look of pleased conjecture. 'And why not?' he wanted to know. 'Mama, will you wait for a few minutes while I see if I can find her? There is no time to explain at the moment—I'll do that later. Shall I ring for a maid before I go?'

It was still raining as he got into the car and slid into the early morning traffic, thickening every minute, but he didn't drive fast. Becky and her companions should be easy enough to see, even in a busy city, but there was always the likelihood that she had gone down some side street. But she hadn't; she had stopped to ask the way to somewhere or other, that was apparent, for the matronly-looking woman she was talking to was pointing down the street. The Baron slid to a halt beside them, wound down his window and said quietly: 'Becky ...'

She turned round at once and when she saw who it was her face broke into a smile. 'Oh, it's you,' she observed. 'Are you on your way again?'

He was disinclined for conversation. 'I have a job for you; you'll have to come back to the hotel, I'll tell you about it there.'

He waited while she thanked the woman and then got out into the rain to usher Bertie in and settle her and Pooch beside him.

As he turned the car, he said severely: 'You are far too trusting, Becky—to accept my word without one single question. I might have been intent on abducting you.'

She gave him a puzzled look. 'But why shouldn't I trust you?' she wanted to know. 'And who in his right mind would want to abduct me?'

'You have a point there.' He threw her a sidelong glance. She looked bedraggled and tired; perhaps his idea hadn't been such a good one after all. On the other hand, some dry clothes and a few good meals might make all the difference. 'That lady you helped in the hotel—she needs a nurse for a few weeks. She liked you, so I said I'd fetch you back so that she could talk to you ...'

'References,' said Becky sadly. 'I haven't any, you know—and I can't prove I'm a nurse.'

He had drawn up before the hotel once more, now he turned to her. 'What would you do if you were given the care of someone with ulcerative protocolitis?'

'Oh, that's usually treated medically, isn't it—they only operate when the disease is severe. I've only seen it done once ...' She launched into a succinct account of what could be done. 'Is that what I'm to nurse?' she asked.

'No. What do you know about serum viral hepatitis?'

She wrinkled her brow. 'I don't know much about that, only that it's transmitted in three ways ...' She mentioned them briefly and he asked quietly:

'The sources?'

She told him those too.

'And what preventative measures can be taken?'

She had to think hard about those, and when she had remembered all six of them she asked: 'Are you examining me?'

'No—You said that you had no references ...'

Becky said suddenly: 'Gosh, how silly I am! You must be a doctor.'

'Indeed I am, and due to leave here within the hour, so if we might go inside ...?'

For all the world as though she had been wasting his time in light conversation, thought Becky. The whole thing must be a dreadful bore for him. With a face like his and a Rolls to boot, he hardly needed to waste time on someone as uninteresting as herself. But she got out obediently, gathered the animals to her, and went back into the hotel.

The little lady she had helped in the foyer turned to stare at her as she entered the room and then took her quite by surprise by exclaiming: 'Yes, that's the one. How very clever of you to find her, Tiele—we'll engage her at once.' Her eyes fell on Bertie and Pooch. 'And these animals ...?'

'I have been thinking about them, Mama, but first

let me introduce you. This is Miss Rebecca Saunders, a registered nurse, who has run away from her home with her two—er—companions. Becky, this is my mother, the Baroness Raukema van den Eck.' So that made him a Baron!

Becky had her mouth open to begin on a spate of questions, but he stopped her with an urgent hand. 'No, there is little time for questions, if you don't mind, I will explain briefly. Pray sit down.'

He was obviously used to having his own way; she sat, with Pooch peering out from under her arm and Bertie on her feet.

'My mother, as you can see for yourself, is for the time being unable to walk. She has a compound fracture of tib and fib which unfortunately has taken some time to knit, and a badly torn semilunar cartilage of the other knee. She has had quadriceps exercises for three weeks with some good results, and we hope she may commence active movement very shortly. When she does so, she will need a nurse to assist her until she is quite accustomed to walking on her plaster, and we are satisfied that the other knee will give no further trouble. As you are aware, she had engaged a nurse to go with her, but this arrangement has fallen through and it is imperative that she has someone now—she will be sailing on a cruise ship from this port late this afternoon. Unfortunately, I have to be back in Holland by tomorrow morning at the latest, which means that I must leave very shortly.' He added, as though it were a foregone conclusion: 'The post should suit you very well.'

Becky sat up straight. 'I should like to ask some

questions,' and at his impatient frown: 'I'll be quick. Where are we going?'

He looked surprised. 'I didn't mention it? Trondheim, in Norway. I have an aunt living there whom my mother wishes to visit.'

'I have no clothes ...'

'Easily remedied. A couple of hours' shopping.'

'What happens when I leave?' She suddenly caught Pooch close so that he let out a raucous protest. 'And what about Pooch and Bertie?' she frowned. 'How can I possibly ...'

'You will return to Holland with my mother where it should be easy enough for you to get a job in one of the hospitals. I shall, of course, give you any help you may need. As to the animals, may I suggest that I take them with me to Holland where they will be well cared for at my home until you return there; after that it should be a simple matter to get a small flat for yourself where they can live.'

'Quarantine?'

'There is none—only injections, which I will undertake to see about.'

It all sounded so easy; she perceived that if you were important and rich enough, most things were easy. All the same she hesitated. 'I'm not sure if they'll like it ...'

He smiled quite kindly then. 'I promise you that they will have the best of treatment and be cared for.'

'Yes, I know, but supposing ...'

'What is the alternative, Becky?' He wasn't smiling now and he sounded impatient again.

The alternative didn't bear thinking about. She

couldn't be sure of getting a job, in the first place, and just supposing she should meet Basil or her step-mother before she had found somewhere to live. He was watching her narrowly. 'Not very attractive, is it?' he asked, 'and you have only enough money for a meal—thirty pounds and—er—sixty pence wouldn't buy you a bed for more than three nights, you know.'

His mother looked at Becky. 'My dear child, is that all the money you have? And why is that? And why did you leave your home?'

'With your permission, Mama; you will have time enough to discuss the whole situation. If Becky could decide—now—there are several matters which I must attend to ...'

She was annoying him now, she could see that, but what seemed so simple from his point of view was an entirely different matter for her. But she would have to agree; the idea of parting with her pets was unpleasant enough, but at least they would be safe and cared for and after a week or so she would be able to collect them and start a new life for herself. To clinch the matter she suddenly remembered the quarantine laws; she would never have enough money to pay the fees—besides, there was no one and nothing to keep her in England. 'Thank you, I'll take the job,' she said in a resolute voice.

'Good, then let us waste no more time. My mother will explain the details later. What fee were you to pay the nurse you dismissed, Mama?'

Son and parent exchanged a speaking glance. 'Sixty pounds a week with—how do you say?—board and lodging.'

'But that's too much!' protested Becky.

'You will forgive me if I remind you that you have been living in, how shall we say? retirement for the past two years. That is the normal pay for a trained nurse working privately. Over and above that you will receive travelling expenses, and a uniform allowance.' He took some notes from a pocket and peeled off several. 'Perhaps you will go now and buy what you think necessary. Your uniform allowance is here, and an advance on your week's pay.'

Becky took the money, longing to count it, but that might look greedy. 'I haven't any clothes,' she pointed out, 'so I'd better buy uniform dresses, hadn't I?'

'Yes, do that, my dear,' interpolated the Baroness. 'You can go shopping in Trondheim and buy the clothes you need.'

Becky found herself in a taxi, the Baron's cool apologies in her ear. He intended leaving at any moment; she was to take a taxi back to the hotel when she had done her shopping. 'And don't be too long about it,' he begged her forthrightly, 'although you don't look to me to be the kind of girl who fusses over her clothes.' A remark which she had to allow was completely justified but hardly flattering. She had bidden Bertie and Pooch goodbye and hated doing it, but they had looked content enough, sitting quietly by the Baroness. At the last moment she poked her head out of the taxi window.

'You will look after them, won't you? They'll be so lonely ...'

'I give you my word, Becky, and remember that in a few weeks' time you will be able to make a home for them.'

She nodded, quite unable to speak for the lump in her throat.

She felt better presently. The Baron didn't like her particularly, she was sure, and yet she felt that she could trust him and upon reflection, she had saved him a lot of time and bother finding another nurse for his mother. She counted the money he had given her and felt quite faint at the amount and then being a practical girl, made a mental list of the things she would need.

It took her just two hours in which to do her shopping; some neat dark blue uniform dresses, because she could wear those each and every day, a blue cardigan and a navy blue raincoat, shoes and stockings and an unassuming handbag and then the more interesting part; undies and a thin dressing gown she could pack easily, and things for her face and her hair. All the same, there was quite a lot of money over. She found a suitcase to house her modest purchases and, obedient to the Baron's wish, took a taxi back to the hotel.

She found her patient lying on a chaise-longue drawn up to the window, a tray of coffee on the table at her elbow. 'I hope I haven't been too long,' began Becky, trying not to look at the corner where Bertie and Pooch had been sitting.

'No, my dear. Tiele went about an hour ago, and your animals went quite happily with him. I must tell you that he has a great liking for animals and they like him.' Her eyes fell upon the case Becky was carrying. 'You bought all that you require?' She nodded to herself without waiting for Becky to reply. 'Then come and have coffee with me and we will get to know each other. Tiele has arranged for us to be taken to the ship in good time; we will have lunch presently—here, I think, as I do dislike being pushed around in that chair—then we shall have time for a rest before we go. I'm sure you must be wondering just where we are going and why,' she added. 'Give me another cup of coffee, child, and I will tell you. I have been staying with an old friend at Blanchland, but unfortunately within two days of arriving I fell down some steps and injured my legs. Tiele came over at once, of course, and saw to everything, and I remained at my friend's house until I was fit to travel again. I could have remained there, but I have a sister living in Trondheim and as I had arranged to visit her before their summer is over, I prevailed upon Tiele to arrange things so that I might go. I get tired in a car and I suffer badly from air-sickness, so he decided that the best plan was for me to go by ship and since there is time enough, to go in comfort and leisure. We shall be sailing to Tilbury first and then to Hamburg and from there to Trondheim, where I intend to stay for three weeks. By then, with your help and that of the local doctor, I should be able to hobble and be out of this wheelchair. I have no idea how we shall return to Holland—Tiele will decide that when the time comes.'

Becky said: 'Yes, of course,' in a rather faint voice. After two years or more of isolation and hard work, events were crowding in on her so that she felt quite bewildered. 'Where do you live in Holland?' she asked.

'Our home is in Friesland, north of Leeuwarden. I don't live with Tiele, of course, now that I am alone

I have moved to a house in Leeuwarden only a few miles from Huis Raukema. I have a daughter, Tialda, who is married and lives in Haarlem. Leeuwarden is a pleasant city, not too large, but you should find work there easily enough—besides, Tiele can help you there.'

'He has a practice in Leeuwarden?'

'Yes, although he doesn't live there.' She put down her cup and saucer. 'I have talked a great deal, but it is pleasant to chat with someone as restful as you are, Becky. I think we shall get on very well together. Tiele says that we must arrange our days in a businesslike fashion, so will you tell me what you think is best?' She opened her bag. 'I almost forgot, he left this for you—instructions, I believe.'

Very precise ones, written in a frightful scrawl, telling her just what he wanted done for his mother, reminding her that she was to take the usual off duty, that she might possibly have to get up at night if the Baroness wasn't sleeping, that she was to report to the ship's doctor immediately she went on board that afternoon and that she was to persevere with active movements however much his mother objected to them. At Trondheim there would be a doctor, already in possession of all the details of his mother's injuries, and he would call very shortly after they arrived there.

He hadn't forgotten anything; organising, she considered, must be his strong point.

'That's all very clear,' she told her patient. 'Shall we go over it together and get some sort of a routine thought out?'

It took them until a waiter came with the lunch

menu. The Baroness had made one or two suggestions which Becky secretly decided were really com-
mands and to which she acceded readily enough,
since none of them were important, but she thought
that they were going to get on very well. The
Baroness was accustomed to having her own way but
she was nice about it. To Becky, who had lived without affection save for her animal friends, her patient
seemed kindness itself. They decided on their lunch
and she got her settled nicely in a chair with a small
table conveniently placed between them and then
went away to change her clothes.

She felt a different girl after she had bathed and
done her hair up into a neat bun and donned the
uniform dress. She had bought some caps too, and
she put one on now and went to join the Baroness,
who studied her carefully, remarking: 'You're far
too thin, Becky, but I like you in uniform. Have you
bought clothes as well?'

'Well, no. You see, I should need such a lot .. :'

Her companion nodded. 'Yes, of course, but there
are some nice shops in Trondheim, you can enjoy
yourself buying all you want there. There's sherry on
the table, child, pour us each a glass and we will wish
ourselves luck.'

Becky hadn't had sherry in ages. It went straight
to her head and made her feel as though life was fun
after all and in a sincere effort not to be thin any
longer, she ate her lunch with a splendid appetite. It
was later, over coffee, that her patient said: 'We have
a couple of hours still. Supposing you tell me about
yourself, Becky?'

CHAPTER TWO

AFTERWARDS, thinking about it, Becky came to the conclusion that she had had far too much to say about herself, but somehow the Baroness had seemed so sympathetic—not that she had said very much, but Becky, who hadn't had anyone to talk to like that for a long time, sensed that the interest was real, as real as the sympathy. She hadn't meant to say much; only that she had trained at Hull because she had always wanted to be a nurse, and besides, her father was a country G.P., and that her mother had died five years earlier and her father three years after her. But when she had paused there her companion had urged: 'But my dear, your stepmother—I wish to hear about her and this so unpleasant son of hers with the funny name ...'

'Basil,' said Becky, and shivered a little. 'He's very good-looking and he smiles a lot and he never quite looks at you. He's cruel; he'll beat a dog and smile while he's doing it. He held my finger in a gas flame once because I'd forgotten to iron a shirt he wanted, and he smiled all the time.'

'The brute! But why were they so unkind to you? How did they treat your father?'

'Oh, they were very nice to him, and of course while he was alive I was at the hospital so I only went home for holidays, and then they persuaded my father to alter his will; my stepmother said that there was no need to leave me anything because she would take care of me and share whatever he left with me. That was a lie, of course. I knew it would be, but I couldn't do much about it, could I?' She sighed. 'And I had already decided that I would get a job abroad. But then Father died and my stepmother told me that I had nothing and that she wasn't going to give me anything and that I wasn't welcome at home any more, but I went all the same because Bertie and Pooch had belonged to my father and I wanted to make sure that they were looked after. We still had the housekeeper Father had before he married again and she took care of them as best she could. And then my stepmother had jaundice. She didn't really need a nurse, but she wrote to the hospital and made it look as though it was vital that I should go home— and then Basil came and told me that they had sacked the housekeeper and that if I didn't go home they'd let Bertie and Pooch starve. So I went home. The house was on the edge of the village and Stoney Chase is a bit isolated anyway. They made it quite clear that I was to take the housekeeper's place, only they didn't pay me any wages to speak of and I couldn't go anywhere, you see, because I had no money after a little while—once I'd used up what I had on things like soap and pantyhose from the village shop . . .'

'You told no one?'

'No. You see, Basil said that if I did he'd kill Pooch

and Bertie, so then I knew I'd have to get away somehow, so each week I kept a bit from the shopping—I had aimed at fifty pounds, but then yesterday Basil and my stepmother were talking and I was in the garden and heard them. He said he was going to drown them both while I was in the village shopping the next day, so then I knew I'd have to leave sooner. We left about three o'clock this morning ...' She had smiled then. 'The doctor stopped and gave us a lift, it was kind of him, especially as he was in such a hurry and we were all so wet and he didn't even know if I was making up the whole thing.' She had added uncomfortably: 'I must have bored you; I hate people who are sorry for themselves.'

'I should hardly say that you were sorry for yourself. A most unpleasant experience, my dear, and one which we must try and erase from your mind. I see no reason why you shouldn't make a pleasant future for yourself when we get to Holland. Nurses are always needed, and with Tiele's help you should be able to find something to suit you and somewhere to live.'

Becky had felt happy for the first time in a long while.

Their removal to the ship took place with an effortless ease which Becky attributed to the doctor's forethought. People materialised to take the luggage, push the wheelchair and get them into a taxi, and at the docks a businesslike man in a bowler hat saw them through Customs and into the hands of a steward on board. Becky, who had visualised a good deal of delay and bother on account of her having no passport, even though the Baroness had assured her that her son had arranged that too, was quite taken aback when the man in the bowler hat handed her a visitor's passport which he assured her would see her safely on her way. She remembered that the doctor had asked her some swift questions about her age and where she was born, but she hadn't taken much notice at the time. It was evident that he was a man who got things done.

The Baroness had a suite on the promenade deck, a large stateroom, a sitting room with a dear little balcony leading from it, overlooking the deck below a splendidly appointed bathroom and a second stateroom which was to be Becky's. It was only a little smaller than her patient's and she circled round it, her eyes round with excitement, taking in the fluffy white towels in the bathroom, the telephone, the radio, the basket of fruit on the table. None of it seemed quite real, and she said so to the Baroness while she made her comfortable and started the unpacking; there was a formidable amount of it; the Baroness liked clothes, she told Becky blandly, and she had a great many. Becky, lovingly folding silk undies which must have cost a fortune and hanging dresses with couture labels, hadn't enjoyed herself so much for years. Perhaps in other circumstances she might have felt envy, but she had a wardrobe of her own to gloat over; Marks & Spencer's undies in place of pure silk, but they were pretty and new. Even her uniform dresses gave her pleasure, and if Bertie and Pooch had been with her she would have been quite happy. She finished the unpacking and went, at her patient's request, to find the purser's office, the shop, the doctor's surgery and the restaurant. 'For you may need to visit all of them at some time or other,' remarked the Baroness, 'and it's so much easier if you know your way around.'

It was a beautiful ship and not overcrowded. Becky, while she was at it, explored all its decks, peeped into the vast ballroom and the various bars and lounges, walked briskly round the promenade deck, skipped to the lowest deck of all to discover the swimming pool and hurried back to her patient, her too thin face glowing with excitement. 'It's super!' she told her. 'You know, I'm sure I could manage the wheelchair if you want to go on deck— I'm very strong.'

The Baroness gave her a faintly smiling look. 'Yes, Becky, I'm sure you are—but what about your sea legs?'

Becky hadn't given that a thought. The sea was calm at the moment, but of course they weren't really at sea yet; they had been passing Tynemouth when she had been on deck, but in another half hour or so they would be really on their way.

'Now let us have some room service,' observed the Baroness. 'Becky, telephone for the stewardess, will you?'

The dark-haired, brown-eyed young creature who presented herself a few minutes later was Norwegian, ready to be helpful and friendly. 'I shall have my breakfast here,' decreed the Baroness, 'and you, Becky, will go to the restaurant for yours.' She made her arrangements smoothly but with great politeness and then asked for the hotel manager, disregarding the stewardess's statement that he wouldn't be available at that time. Becky picked up the telephone once again and passed on the Baroness's request, and was surprised when he actually presented himself within a few minutes.

'A table for my nurse, if you please,' explained the Baroness, and broke off to ask Becky if she wanted to share with other people or sit by herself.

'Oh, alone, please,' declared Becky, and listened while that was arranged to her patient's satisfaction. 'We'll lunch here,' went on Baroness Raukema van den Eck, 'and dine here too.' And when the manager had gone, 'You must have some time to yourself each day—I like a little rest after lunch, so if you settle me down I shall be quite all right until four o'clock or so. I'm sure there'll be plenty for you to do, and I expect you'll make friends.'

Becky doubted that; she had got out of the habit of meeting people and she didn't think anyone would bother much with a rather uninteresting nurse. But she agreed placidly and assured her companion that that would be very nice. 'I've found a library, too,' she said. 'Would you like a book?'

'A good idea—I should. Go and find something for me, my dear, and then we'll have a glass of sherry before dinner. Don't hurry,' she added kindly, 'have a walk on deck as you go.'

It didn't seem like a job, thought Becky, nipping happily from one deck to the other, and it was delightful to be able to talk to someone again. She wondered briefly what the Baron was doing at that moment, then turned her attention to the bookcases.

They dined in the greatest possible comfort with a steward to serve them, and Becky, reading the menu with something like ecstasy, could hardly stop her mouth watering. Her stepmother kept to a strict slimming diet and Basil had liked nothing much but steaks and chops and huge shoulders of lamb; too expensive for more than one, her stepmother had decreed, so that Becky, willy-nilly, had lived on a slimming diet as well, with little chance of adding to her meagre meals because she had to account for the contents of the larder and fridge each morning. Now she ate her way through mushrooms in sauce rémoulade, iced celery soup, cold chicken with tangerines and apple salad, and topped these with peach royale before pouring coffee for them both. She said like a happy little girl: 'That was the best meal I've ever had. I used to think about food a lot, you know, when you're always a bit hungry, you do, but I never imagined anything as delicious as this.' She added awkwardly: 'I don't think you should pay me as much as you said you would, Baroness, because I'm not earning it and I'm getting all this as well ... it doesn't seem quite honest ...'

'You will be worth every penny to me, Becky,' her patient assured her, 'and how you managed to bear with that dreadful life you were forced to lead is more than I can understand. Besides, I am a demanding and spoilt woman, you won't get a great deal of time to yourself.'

Which was true enough. Becky found her day well filled. True, she breakfasted alone in the restaurant, but only after she had spent half an hour with the Baroness preparing that lady for her own breakfast in bed. And then there was the business of helping her patient to dress, getting her into her wheelchair and taking her to whichever part of the ship she preferred. Here they stayed for an hour or so, taking their coffee, chatting a little and enjoying the sun. Becky read aloud too, because the Baroness said it tired her eyes to read for herself, until half an hour or so before lunch when Becky was sent off to walk round the decks or potter round the shop and buy postcards at the purser's office for the Baroness. They were to dock at Tilbury in the morning and as the ship wouldn't sail for Hamburg until the late afternoon the Baroness had suggested that Becky could go up to London and do some shopping and rejoin the ship after lunch. But this Becky declined to do; so far, she considered, she hadn't earned half her salary. She had been hired to look after her patient and that she intended to do. Instead, the two of them spent a peaceful day in the Baroness's stateroom playing bezique, and taking a slow wander round the deck on the quiet ship. But by tea time the passengers were coming aboard and the pair of them retired once more to the little balcony leading from the suite, from where they watched the bustle and to-ing and fro-ing going on below them.

They sailed soon afterwards and Becky, leaving her patient with a considerable pile of mail to read, went on deck to watch the ship leave. She hung over the rails, determined not to miss a thing, and it was half an hour before she tore herself away from watching the busy river scene and returned to the stateroom. The Baroness was telephoning, but she broke off what she was saying to tell Becky: 'It is Tiele—making sure that we are quite all right.' And at Becky's look of surprise: 'He's back in Friesland, and I'm to tell you that Pooch and Bertie have settled down very well.' She nodded dismissal and Becky slipped away to her own cabin.

She had collected all the literature about the voyage that she could lay hands on, and now she sat down and studied it; Hamburg next and then Trondheim. There was a whole day at sea first, though, and more than a day between Hamburg and Trondheim. She began to read the leaflet she had been given and only put it down when her patient called to her through the slightly open door.

At Hamburg the Baroness declared her intention of going ashore. The purser, summoned to the cabin, assured her that a taxi should be arranged without difficulty, that help would be at hand to wheel the chair down the gangway and that the Baroness need have no worry about herself further. To Becky, accustomed to doing everything for herself, it seemed the height of comfort. And indeed, when the ship docked there was nothing for her to do beyond readying her patient for the outing and then walking beside the chair while a steward wheeled it carefully on to the quay. There were several busloads of passengers going on shore excursions and they had been advised by the purser to get back before these returned or the new passengers began to embark. 'Plenty of time,' said the Baroness easily. 'We will drive round the city, take a look at the Binnenalster and the Aussenalster and the driver can take us to a confectioner's so that you can buy me some of the chocolates Tiele always brings me when he comes here.'

She was arranged comfortably in the taxi, accorded a courteous farewell by the officer on duty whom she warned not to allow the ship to leave until her return, and was driven away, with Becky sitting beside her.

It was all very exciting; first the journey through the dock area, which the Baroness didn't bother to look at, but which Becky found absorbing, and then presently the shopping streets and a brief glimpse of the inner lake. 'It is much prettier once we have crossed the Kennedybrucke,' said the Baroness. She said something to the driver in German and he slowed down to take the pleasant road running alongside the lake, its calm water gleaming in the sunshine, the well kept villas in their splendid grounds facing it. Becky's face lighted up and a little colour came into it. 'Oh, this is super!' she declared. 'I had no idea ...'

Her companion cast her a glance full of sympathy, but all she said was: 'I think you will like Trondheim better, although it is a great deal smaller, of course.'

They circled the lake slowly before going back to the shopping centre where the driver parked outside a confectioner's whose windows displayed extravagantly boxed sweets of every sort, and Becky, obedient to her patient's request, went rather hesitantly inside. There were no difficulties, however. She was perfectly understood, her purchases were made and paid for and with several prettily wrapped boxes she got back into the taxi. It surprised her very much when the taxi stopped once more and the driver got out, went into a café and emerged presently with a waiter carrying a tray with coffee and cream cakes. The tray was set carefully upon Becky's knees and they were left to take their elevenses in peace. 'I like

my little comforts,' explained the Baroness placidly.
And get them too, thought Becky admiringly.

Their return to the ship was as smooth as their de-
parture had been. A steward was by the taxi door
almost before it had stopped and the Baroness was
bestowed carefully into her wheelchair once more.
Only when she was quite comfortable did she open
her handbag and pay the driver—generously too, if
the smile on his face was anything to go by. Becky,
trotting along beside the chair, wondered what it
must be like to be rich enough to command all the
attention and comfort one required without apparent
effort. Probably one got used to it and took it as a
matter of course; thinking about it, she remembered
that the Baron hadn't seemed surprised when she had
accepted the job he had offered her out of the blue.
She was deeply grateful to him, of course, but at the
same time she couldn't help wondering what he
would have done if she had refused.

The Baroness was tired after their outing, so she
elected to take a light lunch in her stateroom and
then rest, sending Becky down to the restaurant for
her own lunch while she ate hers. Becky found the
place quite full, for a good many more passengers
had boarded the ship that morning. She sat at her
table, set discreetly in a corner, and ate a rather
hurried meal, in case the Baroness should want her
the minute she had finished her own lunch, and then
slipped away, smiling rather shyly at the waiter as
she did so. She hadn't quite got used to being waited
on.

The Baroness was drinking her coffee but pro-
fessed herself quite ready to rest. Becky made her

comfortable on the sofa along one wall, covered her with a rug and sat down nearby because her patient had asked her not to go away for a little while. 'I'm expecting a call from Tiele,' explained the Baroness, 'and if you would stay until it comes through ...' She closed her eyes and dozed while Becky sat, still as a mouse, listening to the exciting noises going on all around them—people talking, music coming from somewhere, but faintly, the winch loading the luggage, an occasional voice raised in command or order. It was all very exciting; she contemplated her new shoes and thought about the Baron, his mother, the journey they were about to make, Norway, about which she knew almost nothing, and then the Baron again. It was a pity he didn't like her, but very understandable, and it made his kindness in taking care of Bertie and Pooch all the greater; it couldn't be much fun doing kindnesses to someone you didn't care a row of pins for. Her thoughts were interrupted by the faint tinkle of the telephone, and she picked it up quickly with a glance at the still sleeping Baroness. Her hullo was quiet and the Baron said at once: 'Becky? My mother's asleep?'

'Yes, but I think she would like me to wake her, if you would wait a moment.'

He didn't answer her but asked: 'You're settling down, I hope? No snags? You won't give way to seasickness or anything of that sort, I hope?' She heard him sigh. 'You didn't look very strong.'

Becky's voice stayed quiet but held indignation. 'I'm very strong,' she told him quite sharply, 'and as the sea is as calm as a millpond, I'm not likely to be seasick.'

'You seem to have a temper too,' remarked the Baron. 'As long as you don't vent it on my mother ...'

'Well,' breathed Becky, her chest swelling with rage under the neat dress, 'I never did! As though I would! And I haven't got a temper ...'

'I'm glad to hear it. Bertie and Pooch are quite nicely settled.'

'I'm so glad—I've been worrying about them just a little; you're sure ...?'

'Quite. Now if you would wake up my mother, Nurse?'

She was to be nurse, was she? And what was she to call him? Baron or doctor or sir? She crossed the room and roused the Baroness with a gentle touch on her shoulder and that lady opened her eyes at once with a look of such innocence that Becky didn't even begin to suspect that her patient had been listening to every word she had uttered.

She went to her cabin while mother and son carried on a quite lengthy conversation and spent ten minutes or so doing things to her face. She had bought make-up, the brand she had always used when she had money of her own to spend, and now she was enjoying the luxury of using it. She applied powder to her small nose, lipstick to her too large mouth, and tidied her hair under her cap and then studied her face. Nothing remarkable; no wonder her employer had dismissed her with the kind of casual kindness he would afford a stray cat. She sighed and then adjusted her expression to a cheerful calm at the sound of her patient's voice calling her.

The rest of the day passed pleasantly enough with the Baroness remarkably amenable when called upon to do her exercises. The moment they got on shore at Trondheim, Becky had been told to instruct her in the use of crutches, something she wasn't looking forward to over-much. The Baroness could be a trifle pettish if called upon to do something she didn't fancy doing, and yet Becky already liked her; she had probably spent a spoilt life with a doting husband and now a doting son, having everything she wanted within reason, but she could be kind too and thoughtful of others, and, Becky reminded herself, she had a wonderful job; well paid, by no means exhausting and offering her the chance of seeing something of the world.

There were almost two days before they would arrive at Trondheim, and Becky found that they went too quickly. A good deal of time was spent on deck, the Baroness in her wheelchair, Becky sitting beside her while they carried on a gentle flow of small talk. There was plenty to talk about; the distant coastline of Sweden and then Norway, their fellow passengers, the day's events on board; there was so much to do and even though neither of them took part in any of them, it was fun to discuss them. The Captain was giving a cocktail party that evening, but the Baroness had declared that nothing would persuade her to go to it in a wheelchair; they would dine quietly in her stateroom as usual, and Becky didn't mind; she had nothing to wear and the idea of appearing at such a glittering gathering in a nurse's uniform didn't appeal to her in the least. All the same, it would have been fun to have seen some of the dresses . . .

The Baroness liked to dress for the evening. Becky, helping her into a black chiffon gown and laying a

lacy shawl over her knees, wished just for a moment
that they had been going to the party, it seemed such
a waste . . .

It wasn't a waste. Instead of the sherry which the
steward brought to the stateroom, he carried a bottle
of champagne in an ice bucket, and following hard
on his heels was the Captain himself, accompanied
by several of his officers, and they were followed by
more stewards bearing trays of delicious bits and
pieces, presumably to help the champagne down.
Becky, with a young officer on either side of her, intent on keeping her glass filled and carrying on the
kind of conversation she had almost forgotten
existed, found life, for the first time in two years, was
fun.

When the gentlemen had gone the Baroness sat
back in her chair and eyed Becky. 'You must buy
yourself some pretty clothes,' she observed. 'You
won't always be on duty, you know—I know there
was no time in Newcastle to do more than get the
few essentials, but once we are in Trondheim you
shall go shopping. Tiele gave you enough money, I
hope?'

Becky thought with still amazed astonishment of
the notes in her purse. 'More than enough,' she explained. 'A week's salary in advance and money to
buy my uniforms and—and things.'

'A week's salary? What is that? Let me see, sixty
pounds, did we not say? What is sixty pounds?' It
was lucky that she didn't expect an answer, for Becky
was quite prepared to tell her that for her, at least, it
was a small fortune. 'When we get to Trondheim you
will have your second week's wages—not very much,

but I daresay you will be able to find something to wear.'

Becky thought privately that she would have no difficulty at all, although she had no intention of spending all that money. It was of course tempting to do so, but she had the future to think of; she supposed her present job would last a month or a little longer and even though she managed to get another job at once, there would be rent to pay if she were lucky enough to find somewhere to live, and food for herself and the animals until she drew her pay. All the same she allowed herself the luxury of planning a modest outfit or two. They would arrive at Trondheim the next day and a little thrill of excitement ran through her, just for the moment she forgot the future and the unpleasant past; Norway, as yet invisible over the horizon, was before her and after that Holland. Perhaps later she would be homesick for England, but now she felt secure and content, with almost the width of the North Sea between her and her stepmother and Basil.

She fell to planning the little home she would make for herself and Bertie and Pooch and was only disturbed in this pleasant occupation by the Baroness, who had been reading and now put down her book and suggested a game of dominoes before the leisurely process of getting ready for bed.

The next day was fine and warm, the sea was calm and very blue and the shores of Norway, towering on either side of the Trondheimsfjord, looked magnificent. Becky, released from the patient's company for an hour, hung over the rail, not missing a thing; the tiny villages in the narrow valleys, the farms perched

impossibly on narrow ledges half way up the mountains with apparently no way of reaching them, the
camping sites on the edge of the water and the cosy
wooden houses. It was only when Trondheim came
into sight, still some way off on a bend of the fjord,
that she went reluctantly back to the Baroness. She
had packed earlier, there was little left to do other
than eat their lunch and collect the last few odds and
ends, but there would be ample time for that; the
Baroness had elected to wait until the passengers
who were going on the shore excursions had left the
ship; they would have to go ashore by tender, and
Becky knew enough of her patient by now to guess
that that lady avoided curious glances as much as
possible.

The passengers were taken ashore with despatch
and wouldn't return until five o'clock. Becky, sent on
deck to take a breath of air while her patient enjoyed
a last-minute chat with the ship's doctor, the purser
and the first officer, watched the last tender returning from the shore. Trondheim looked well worth a
visit and she longed to get a closer look. It was nice
to think that she would have two or three weeks in
which to explore it thoroughly. There was a lot to
see; the cathedral, the old warehouses, the royal
palace, the Folk Museum ... she pitied the passengers who had just gone ashore and who would have
to view all these delights in the space of a few hours.
One of the young officers who had come to the
Baroness's cabin joined her at the rail. 'You get off
here, don't you?' he asked in a friendly voice. He
glanced at her trim uniform. 'Will you get time to
look around Trondheim?—it's a lovely old place.'

'Oh, I'm sure I shall—I don't have to work hard, you know. The Baroness is kindness itself and I get free time each day just like anyone else.' She smiled at him. 'I loved being on board this ship.'

He smiled back at her; he was a nice young man with a pretty girl at home waiting to marry him and he felt vague pity for this small plain creature, who didn't look plain at all when she smiled. He said now: 'Well, I hope you enjoy your stay in Norway. Do you go back to Holland with the Baroness?'

'Yes, just for a little while, then I'll get a job there.'

He looked at her curiously. 'Don't you want to go back to England?'

She was saved from answering him by the stewardess coming in search of her to tell her that the Baroness was ready to go ashore now. Getting that lady into the tender was a delicate operation involving careful lifting while Becky hovered over the plastered leg, in a panic that the tender would give a lurch and it would receive a thump which would undo all the good it had been doing. But nothing happened, the Baroness was seated at last, the leg carefully propped up before her and Becky beside her, their luggage was stowed on board, and they made the short trip to the shore. Here the same procedure had to be carried out, although it wasn't quite as bad because there were no stairs to negotiate. Becky nipped on to the wooden pier and had the wheelchair ready by the time the Baroness was borne ashore. Escorted by a petty officer, they made their way off the pier to the land proper.

There were a lot of people about and a couple of officials who made short work of examining their papers before waving them on to where a Saab Turbo was waiting. The lady sitting in the car got out when she saw them coming, not waiting for her companion, and ran to meet them. She was a small woman, a little older than the Baroness and very like her in looks. The two ladies embraced, both talking at once, and only broke off when the elderly gentleman who had been in the car reached them. The Baroness embraced him too and embarked on another conversation to stop in the middle of a sentence and say in English: 'I am so excited, you must forgive me, I had forgotten my dear Becky. She has looked after me so very well and she is going to stay with me until I return home.' She turned to Becky standing quietly a few paces away. 'Becky, come and meet my sister and brother-in-law. Mijnheer and Mevrouw van Denne—he is Consul here and will know exactly the right places for you to see while you are here. And now if I could be put in the car ...?'

An oldish man joined them and was introduced as Jaap the chauffeur, between them Becky and he lifted the Baroness into the back seat where she was joined by the Consul and his wife while Becky, having seen the chair and the luggage safely stowed in the boot, got in beside Jaap.

She tried to see everything as they went through the city, of course, but she would have needed eyes all round her head. But she glimpsed two department stores and a street of pleasant shops with other streets leading from it and she had the palace pointed out to her, an imposing building built entirely of wood, then they were in a wide street with the cathedral at its far end. But they didn't get as far as that; half way down

Jaap turned into a tree-lined avenue with large houses, before one of which he slowed to turn again into a short drive and stop before its solid front door. They had arrived. Becky drew a deep breath to calm herself. It would never do to get too excited; she was a nurse and must preserve a calm front, but her eyes shone with delight and her pale face held a nice colour for once. The Baroness, watching her with some amusement, decided that she wasn't only a nice girl, she was—just now and again—quite a pretty one, too.

CHAPTER THREE

THE house was surprisingly light inside and furnished with large, comfortable furniture. The whole party crossed the hall and went into a lofty sitting room with a splendid view of the cathedral in the distance, and the Baroness, still talking, was transferred from her wheelchair to a high-backed winged chair while coffee and little cakes were served by a cheerful young woman whom the Baroness's sister introduced as Luce. She added, smiling at Becky, 'And you do not mind if we call you Becky?' Her English was as good as her sister's.

'Please do,' said Becky, and was interrupted by her patient with : 'And tomorrow morning, my dear, you shall go to the shops as soon as you have helped me, and buy yourself some pretty clothes. It is a good idea to wear uniform, I know, but now you will get some free time each day and then you will want to go out and enjoy yourself.'

Her three companions turned to look at her kindly, but she could also see doubt in their elderly faces. If she had been pretty, she thought wryly, she would probably have a simply super time, as it was she would have to content herself with a round of museums and

48

places of interest. She gave herself a mental shake, appalled at her self-pity; good fortune was smiling on her at last, and she had no need to be sorry for herself. She agreed with enthusiasm tempered with a reminder that exercises for the day hadn't yet been done and since the family doctor was going to call that evening, it might be as well if they were done and over before he arrived—a remark which was the signal to convey the Baroness to her room on the ground floor. It was a charming apartment and extremely comfortable with a bathroom leading from it and on the other side of that, a smaller but just as comfortable room for Becky. The exercises over, she settled her patient back into a chair by the window and prepared to unpack, a task which was frequently interrupted by her companion who was watching the traffic in the distance and declared that she could see the coachloads of passengers off the ship on their way to the cathedral. 'You must go there,' she declared. 'It is quite beautiful—I should like to see it again myself.'

'Then we'll go together,' said Becky instantly. 'It's no distance. I'll push the chair—the exercise will do me good.'

The Baroness was doubtful. 'Tiele said that you weren't to do too much heavy lifting—he seems to think you're not very strong.'

Becky gave a snort. 'Then he's mistaken—I'm as strong as a horse! When I was at home I used to do almost all the housework; it was quite a big house, too, with miles of flagstoned floors and stairs to polish and heavy furniture to shift about.'

'Disgraceful!' the Baroness sounded indignant.

'Your stepmother should be brought to justice for treating you in such a way.' She considered a moment. 'Of course, the maids at home have a good deal of housework to do, but they are well paid and none of them is overworked.' She turned away from the window and watched Becky hanging a black velvet dress in the wardrobe. 'What clothes will you buy?'

'Well, I thought a couple of cotton dresses because it's warm, isn't it? I thought it would be much cooler ...'

'It can be cool, but a cotton dress or two could be useful—get a jacket or something to wear with them —what else?'

'Slacks? Some thin tops, perhaps a sweater, some light shoes or sandals ...'

'A pretty dress for the evening, of course. Two.'

Becky, who hadn't had a new dress for so long, heaved a sigh of great content.

The Baroness was unusually docile the following morning; she allowed Becky to assist her to dress, did her exercises with exemplary perfection, the while discussing Doctor Iversen's visit. He had come just before dinner on the previous evening and he knew so much about the Baroness's injuries that Becky felt sure that the Baron had taken care to give him every last detail. He applauded her progress, agreed that the exercises should be stepped up and went away again, promising to call in two days' time bringing with him some gutter crutches so that the Baroness might start to walk again. 'The quicker you are on your feet the better,' he had pointed out. 'You are here for two—three weeks? Then by the time you leave us, Baroness, I believe you will be able to manage very well.' He had given Becky one or two instructions in his excellent English, and smiled at her very kindly.

Becky walked to the shops. The city was spread widely and easy to find one's way about. There were two department stores, Mevrouw van Denne had told her—Sundt & Co in Kongens Gate and Steen & Strom, Olav Tryggvasonsgate, fairly close to each other. She prowled happily round them in turn and finally returned to the Consul's house, laden with parcels, all of which she had to undo and display their contents to the Baroness, who had been stationed strategically in the hall, waiting for her. Two cotton dresses and a cardigan to go with them, blue slacks and a couple of cotton tops, sensible flat sandals and a pair of pretty slippers, a flowered cotton skirt and a lace-trimmed blouse to go with it, and a pale green jersey dress, very simple but, as the Baroness remarked approvingly: 'In excellent taste.' She added: 'Is that all, Becky?'

Becky had spent just about all the money she had, but she didn't say so. When she had her next pay she would buy another dress perhaps, but from now on she was determined to save as much as she could. Her job here in Norway was more like a holiday; once she got to Holland and got work in a hospital there she would need all the money she could spare— there would be food for herself and the animals, lodgings and light and heating and all the other mundane things which cost money; besides, the clothes she had bought had been rather expensive. 'I'll look around,' she told the Baroness placidly, 'and when I

see something nice I'll buy it,' a statement with which
the Baroness was in complete agreement since that
was something she had always been able to do herself.

The Baron telephoned again that evening and this
time Becky was called to speak to him. She faithfully
relayed Doctor Iversen's remarks, assured him that
his mother was doing very nicely and was surprised,
when she had finished, to be asked if she was enjoying herself and having enough time in which to see
the city for herself.

She told him she had plenty of free time and enquired about Bertie and Pooch. 'They're in excellent
condition and perfectly happy. Have you had a free
day yet, Becky?'

'Me? No—what would I do with it?' she asked him
in a matter-of-fact voice. 'I'm very happy, and the
Baroness is a perfect patient.'

Which wasn't quite true; her patient liked her own
way and was used to getting it and she could be imperious at times, but Becky liked her. The work
wasn't arduous; she considered that she was overpaid
and the question of a day off hadn't entered her
mind.

'You will probably meet someone of your own
age,' persisted the Baron, 'and wish to spend a day
with them—there are some interesting trips you can
make ...'

'I don't think I'll meet anyone—in any case,' she
reminded him severely, 'I'm not on holiday, you
know.'

But during the next week or so it seemed as though
she was. True, the Baroness took up the major por-

tion of her day; the crutches had to be mastered and
since her patient had taken exception to them on the
grounds that they were clumsy and ugly, it took a
good deal of coaxing to get her to use them. But after
the first few days she began to make progress,
although her confidence was so small that she refused
to go anywhere, even across the room, without Becky
beside her, but as there was a constant stream of visitors to the house, Becky was able to get an hour here
and an hour there. She met people too. The Consul
lived fairly quietly, but there was a good deal of coming and going between the Consulates, small dinner
parties, coffee in the morning, people dropping in for
tea in the afternoons, and since the Baroness couldn't
go out to any great extent, the visits were more frequent. The Baroness was meticulous in introducing
Becky to anyone and everyone who called, and despite her protests, she attended all the dinner parties
and was treated more like a daughter of the house
than a nurse. And she was liked by everyone too,
although she didn't realise that herself. As the
Baroness said to her sister: 'Becky may be a plain
girl, but she has charm and a restful manner and the
sweetest smile. She is also a splendid nurse. I must
tell Tiele to see that she gets a really good job when
we get back. The child deserves it after these last few
wretched years.'

The two ladies, quite carried away, discussed the
matter at some length.

Becky, true to her promise, took the Baroness to
the cathedral. It was a bright sunny day and not too
warm and the journey there wasn't too arduous. The
Nidras Cathedral loomed before them, its dark

granite exterior almost forbidding. It was dark inside,
too, but its beautiful windows softened the darkness
to a dim peace which Becky found soothing as well
as awe-inspiring. And once inside they joined one of
the groups of visitors being led round by students,
picturesque in their long red gowns, addressing their
audiences with apparently no difficulty at all in whatever language was needed. Becky, on the fringe of
their group because of the awkwardness of the wheelchair, missed a good deal of what was said and made
up her mind to go again, on her own, and this she was
able to do the very next day when several ladies came
for coffee and she was dismissed kindly by the
Baroness and told to go and enjoy herself until lunch
time. And this time she kept well to the fore in the
group following the guide so that she missed nothing
at all, inspecting the Gothic interior to her heart's
content, treading the dark passages behind the altar
to see the spring in the walls and then going all round
the outside to admire the great building. It gave her a
taste for sightseeing and after that she visited the
wooden houses along the waterfront and the *veits*, the
narrow medieval lanes between the main streets, as
well as paying a visit to Stiftsgaarden, the large
wooden palace in the middle of the city. There was
only one place she hadn't managed to visit; the Folk
Museum on the outskirts of Trondheim. It was too
far to walk in the brief periods of freedom she had
and even if she treated herself to a taxi she would be
worrying all the time that she would be late back; the
Baroness was a dear, but she liked everyone to be
punctual, although it wasn't one of her own virtues.

The Baron telephoned regularly, sometimes asking

to speak to her, but more often than not sending some casual message about Bertie and Pooch. In another week they would be going to Holland and she could hardly wait to see her old friends again, although she felt regret that she had seen so little of Norway. She had loved every minute of it and she had been luckier than she had deserved. The thought of a new job and freedom went to her head like strong drink, so that she bought a knitted top and skirt in a pleasing shade of old rose, just because she found it pretty. She tried it on again that evening when she was getting ready for bed and pranced around her room, her mousey hair done in an elaborate whirl and her best shoes on her feet. Life was fun, she told herself.

It was still fun in the morning; it was glorious weather and she put on her uniform dress and cap with something like regret; a cotton dress would have been so much more suitable, but the Baroness had old-fashioned ideas about nurses; she liked Becky in uniform unless she was free. She perched her cap tidily, made sure that her face was nicely made up and went along the hall as was her custom to get the post for the Baroness and fetch the coffee tray which would be in readiness on the sitting room table. It was still early, barely eight o'clock, and the house was quiet. She whistled softly as she went and, still whistling, opened the sitting-room door.

The last person she had expected to see was standing in the big bay window, hands in the pockets of his beautifully cut trousers, looking out into the street. He turned as she paused in the doorway and gave her a long, considering look. 'Good morning, Becky,' said the Baron.

'Well!' said Becky, and was annoyed to find herself blushing. 'Good morning—I didn't expect to see you ...'

'Why should you?' he asked coolly. 'I didn't tell you I was coming.' He smiled across the room, not at her but at someone else. He wasn't alone; there was a tall, graceful girl sitting on the arm of a chair in a corner of the large room. She was wearing slacks and a loosely belted tunic and looked exactly as Becky longed to look and never did. She was pretty too, with strong features and bright blue eyes, and when she turned them on Becky it was very plain to see that she was the Baron's sister. She smiled now in a friendly way while the Baron contented himself with a brief glance before turning his head to look out of the window again.

'You're surprised to see us,' he commented idly. 'Tialda, this is Becky, who is looking after Mama.' He nodded vaguely in his sister's direction. 'Becky, this is my sister Tialda.'

Becky said how do you do and pondered her reason for feeling so relieved when she had realised that it was the Baron's sister and not some girl-friend; she had no reason to feel relief. She frowned a little and the Baron said briskly: 'We have decided to take a short holiday here.'

'Oh? Well, that's nice.' Becky felt the inadequacy of her words and beamed at them warmly to make up for it.

The girl's smile deepened. 'You said she was plain,' she observed to her brother. 'A half starved mouse.'

He gave Becky another look. 'And so she was—it must be the food and the fresh air.' He gave Becky a bland smile. 'You filled out very nicely, Becky.'

He was impossible! Becky hated him, although she didn't hate him in the same way as she hated Basil. There was a difference, like hating a thunderstorm and something nasty under an upturned stone ...

'If you have finished discussing me,' she said haughtily, 'I'll tell the Baroness that you're here.' At the door she paused to say: 'Such manners!'

Tialda crossed the room and tucked an arm under her brother's. 'And that puts you in your place, my boy.' She looked up at him. 'We were abominably rude, you know—I shall apologise; I think she's rather a sweetie.'

He smiled down at her. 'Yes? She would be disappointed if I did. She is grateful—rather touchingly so—because I rescued her, but that doesn't prevent her having a rather poor opinion of me. I fancy that I'm overbearing as well as rude and too much given to getting my own way.'

'What a nice change from girls melting all over you, though you're quite nice really.'

Tialda turned round as the door opened and Becky came in. 'The Baroness would like you to go in immediately,' she announced in a cold little voice. 'It's the door on the right of the stairs. Would you like your coffee with her or later?'

Tialda had crossed the room to stand before her. 'I'm sorry I was rude,' she said gently, 'it was unforgivable of me; you've been so kind to Mama, I hope you'll not mind too much.' She held out an exquisitely manicured hand. 'I should like to be friends.'

Becky took the hand in her own small capable one.

She said rather gruffly: 'I don't mind a bit, really I don't, especially as it was true. And it would be nice to be friends.' She looked up and caught the Baron's eye fixed on her and saw the mocking light in it.

He threw up a protesting hand and said silkily: 'Don't look at me like that, Becky—I have no manners, you know.'

But when she saw him next he wasn't silky at all, he was impersonally polite, just like a consultant doing a round of a ward; it was 'If you please, Nurse,' or 'Lift the leg, will you, Nurse?' or 'Be so good as to hand me that tendon hammer, Nurse.' Just as though he'd never seen her before in his life! And she for her part behaved exactly as she sensed he expected her to, a quiet, well-trained nurse, only speaking when spoken to, anticipating his wants a split second before he voiced them, waiting ready with the crutches so that his mother could demonstrate her progress, re-bandaging the injured knee with neat speediness ... Doctor Iversen was there too, and the two men conferred together, occasionally turning to her for information while the Baroness sat on a chair between them, looking impatient. At length she asked with some asperity:

'Well, will you not tell me how I progress? All this solemn talk ... is it so necessary? I am a little bored.' She glanced at Becky. 'I expect Becky is too, but of course she has been trained not to show it.'

Her son laughed at her. 'Allow us a little self-importance, Mama,' he begged, 'and yes, we're delighted with your progress. You have done very well indeed, there's no reason why you shouldn't use your leg normally provided you're careful—you'll have to wear a supporting bandage for a little longer, of course, and in a couple of weeks the plaster on the other leg can come off. We'll see to that when we get home.' He looked at Becky. 'I hope you will stay with my mother for a week or so in Holland—just until she can walk with a stick. It will give you time to get another job, too.'

Becky said yes, thank you, relieved that she would have a little time in which to get used to the idea of working in a foreign land and to find herself somewhere to live. She did a few rapid sums in her head and decided that she wouldn't buy anything else but save every penny. Rent in advance, she thought worriedly, and food and probably bus fares ... 'Becky,' said the Baron softly, and she realised that he had said her name several times. 'I was only saying,' he said patiently, 'that the exercises might be lengthened considerably ...'

She was kept busy for the rest of the morning. The Baroness was excited and impatient and wanted to skip her usual routine, which Becky wouldn't allow, but she recovered her good humour presently when everyone gathered for drinks before lunch and over that meal she dominated the table with her amusing conversation, and afterwards she declared that she would have her rest in the drawing room so that she could gossip with Tialda, and Becky could have an hour off and go to Sundt and match up the embroidery silks. 'And don't be long, my dear,' she added. 'You said you would massage my shoulders.'

Becky whisked away, changed into one of the cotton dresses and walked to the shops. She would have liked more time; it was exactly the kind of weather in which to take a long walk—she could have gone down to the harbour and watched the coastline express come in, a daily event of which she never tired; it fired her imagination that the miniature liner went to and fro together with its sister ships every day of the year, whatever the weather, calling at each small village all the way to Kirkenes on the very border of Russia. One day, she promised herself, she would make the journey, but now she did her errand and hurried back, to thread the Baroness's needle because the little lady declared that her eyesight was worsening and then go to her room to fetch a shawl she wanted Tialda to see. It was after their afternoon tea, while Becky was encouraging the Baroness to put her weight on the almost sound leg, that her son joined them, and presently, when the exercises were finished and the Baroness was sitting once more and Becky had gone to find Tialda so that her mother could continue their pleasant chat, he asked: 'Has Becky had any days off, Mama? You have been here two weeks as well as several days on board ship.'

The Baroness looked unhappy. 'Oh, dear—I did tell you that I would see that she had a day, or was it two—each week, but somehow I forgot, and she is such a sweet little thing and such good company ... she has had several hours each day, though, most afternoons, you know.'

'And have you had to rouse her at night, my dear?'

'Once or twice—if I have wanted a drink or could not sleep.' She looked a little shamefaced. 'Have I been selfish, Tiele?'

He bent to kiss her cheek. 'No, my dear, but I think we might arrange a few days for her, don't you agree?

I was talking to Iversen, he knows of a nurse who will come in each day and look after you while Becky has her little holiday.'

'Of course, dear. But where will she go?'

The Baron got to his feet and strolled to the window. 'Tialda thinks it might be a good idea if we drove over to Molde and took Becky with us. For three—perhaps four days, and when we come back she can get you ready to come back with us. Do you think you could manage the car journey if we spend three nights on the way? We'll make you comfortable in the back of the car and you'll have Becky.'

'I shall enjoy it,' declared his parent. 'Is it very far?'

'Seven hundred miles, perhaps a little more. We'll stop whenever you're tired and we can cross from Kristiansand to Hirtshals and drive down from there.'

'I wonder what Becky will say?' asked his mother.

'I'll let her know this evening,' he said carelessly. 'I thought we might go tomorrow—it's only a hundred and seventy miles or so. We can leave after lunch—I don't suppose she'll need much time to put a few things in a bag.'

The Baroness looked at him thoughtfully. 'No,' she said at length, 'the child has pitifully few things to put into a bag, she has bought almost no clothes since we have been here.'

'Very sensible of her. She's presumably saving for her future comfort.'

'Don't you like her?'

He laughed gently. 'It depends what you mean by that, Mama. I like Becky, she's a good nurse, and she's gone through a nasty patch, but she's hardly a beauty, is she? and her conversation hardly sparkles. Shall we say that she's not quite my type—I'm not attracted to thin mice.'

It was a pity that Becky heard him as she came back into the room. The self-confidence she had so painfully built up since she had been with the Baroness oozed out of her sensible shoes and her face went rigid in an effort to compose it to a suitably unaware expression. She was aware that she was being looked at quite searchingly, but her voice was nicely normal as she informed her patient that Tialda would join them in a few minutes. She didn't look at the Baron at all, but murmured some vague nothing at the Baroness and made for the door. The Baron reached it at the same time, held it open for her and followed her into the hall, shutting the door behind him. 'A few words with you?' he suggested, and Becky, boiling with rage and humiliation behind her quiet face, said 'certainly' in a voice just as quiet. It seemed likely that he was going to give her the sack or at least express displeasure at something or other. After all, she had just heard him ... her face didn't alter, but her eyes spoke volumes.

'No, you're not getting the sack,' observed the Baron disconcertingly. 'On the contrary, I am delighted with my mother's progress and the care you have given her—she never ceases to sing your praises. You have had no days off, I believe? I'm sorry about that, my mother forgot about them, but you shall have them at once. Tialda and I are going to drive over to Molde for a few days tomorrow, and we should like you to come with us. We shall leave after lunch.'

Becky stared at his tie, because that was on a level with her eyes. Nothing, she told herself fiercely, would make her do any such thing—the arrogance of the man, throwing her a holiday with the careless concern of one throwing a bone to a hungry dog! She went bright pink and said: 'No, thank you,' in a tight voice.

'Oh—why not?' He spoke easily as though he didn't much mind.

'You wouldn't enjoy my company.'

'Probably not,' he sounded amused, 'but Tialda wants you to come, you'll be company for each other and leave me in peace.'

Becky eyed him thoughtfully. He might have saved her from Basil and her stepmother, but she couldn't for the life of her think why. She perceived then that she was a convenience to him; his sister had looked considerably younger than he, it was more than likely that he would be glad to share her society with someone else. She couldn't very well refuse—besides, he had been the means of her starting a new life as well as saving Bertie and Pooch from a horrid fate. 'When do you want me to be ready?' she asked.

'Sensible girl! After lunch tomorrow. Don't bother with clothes, something to travel in and a dress for the evening.'

Which was about all she had anyhow.

They left immediately after lunch the following day with brother and sister sitting together and Becky, looking small and a little lost, in the back of the Rolls. She had had a busy morning, explaining just how the Baroness liked things done, to the Norwegian nurse who was to take her place while she was away—a very pretty girl with excellent English and dark curly hair. The Baron had talked to her for quite a time and as they drove away from the house he remarked: 'Margarethe seems a charming girl, Mama will enjoy her company. Come to that, I'd quite enjoy her company myself.'

Tialda laughed and Becky, who had had a glass of claret with her lunch as well as sherry before it and was feeling quite reckless in consequence, observed tartly: 'Quite your type in fact, Baron Raukema.'

His eye caught and held hers in the mirror above his seat. 'I wondered if you overheard me yesterday. It seems that you did.' She stared at him like a mesmerised rabbit and only a sudden spate of traffic saved her, as he had to keep his eyes on the road.

But that was all he said about it. Presently, free of Trondheim and on the road south, he began to tell her about the country they were passing through and with Tialda joining in, the conversation seemed nothing but a rather lighthearted resumé of their holiday, to which Becky added only a guarded remark from time to time. But presently she began to relax. Tialda was full of fun, telling her of their previous holidays in Molde: 'Winter sports, you know, Becky—we have been several times; last year we came with my husband, Pieter.' She sighed loudly. 'He is away in America for a few weeks and I miss him.' The sigh turned to a laugh. 'I have to put up with Tiele instead and he is only a brother, you understand.'

They were driving quite fast now through magnificent country, the Rolls making light of the steep road and the hairpin bends. 'Where shall we stop for tea?' asked the Baron. 'I told the hotel we'd get there some time before dinner; we've time enough, although the road climbs a bit presently.'

Becky, looking a little nervously out of the window, considered that the road was doing that already. She didn't fancy heights, but there was so much to see and with Tialda keeping up a continuous chatter, she had no time to worry about that. The Baron's blue eyes encountered hers once more in the mirror. 'Enjoying it?' he wanted to know.

'Oh, yes, it's—it's—I've never seen anything like it.' The words were commonplace enough, but her eyes shone with excitement and there was a faint colour in her cheeks. She had washed her hair the night before and now, tied back neatly, it hung in a pale brown cloud round her shoulders, making her eyes look darker than they really were and although her cotton dress was ordinary enough, it was a pretty green check which showed up her creamy skin. She looked a very different girl from the waif he had encountered and befriended, thought Tiele; he must remember to see that she got a good job when they got back ...

Becky stared out at the towering mountains. She was getting used to the scenery now and she had no reason to feel nervous. The Baron was a superb driver, taking no risks but keeping up a good speed with nonchalant calm while Tialda kept up a ceaseless stream of chatter; what they would do, where they would go, what they would buy. 'You've no idea how glad I am to have you here, Becky,' she remarked happily. 'You see, I've just started a baby and Tiele wouldn't have any idea what to do if anything were to go wrong ...'

'But the—the Baron is a doctor,' exclaimed Becky.

'Not that kind of a doctor. He's a physician— hearts and lungs and things.'

'Oh, I see,' said Becky politely. She saw very well. She was still the nurse in the Baron's employ—he might call it days off, but she had merely switched from one patient to the other. She glanced at the broad back in front of her and frowned at it. He was a domineering man who was manipulating her to suit himself under the guise of the generous offer of a holiday. She should have felt very angry, but all she felt was very sad.

They stopped for tea at an hotel built on a terrifying curve half way up a mountain, and Becky was surprised at its luxurious appearance. It wasn't all that large, but it was built in a chalet style and there was a lake behind it in whose steel blue waters the mountains were reflected. She paused at the door to take in the view while Tialda hurried inside, intent on tea, and the Baron, who had been with her, turned back and came to stand beside Becky. 'It's not like that at all,' he explained in a gentle voice which took her by surprise. 'I haven't brought you along for convenience, and strange though it may seem, I am quite capable of dealing with any emergency which Tialda might spring on me. You're here for a short holiday, Becky—I want you to enjoy it.'

'You don't like thin mice,' Becky reminded him coldly.

His eyes twinkled and his smile very nearly made her change her mind about him. 'I'm not sure about that any more.' He eyed her without haste. 'And you aren't so thin, you know.'

He took her arm and turned her round and walked her into the hotel where they found Tialda happily deciding which of the splendid array of cakes offered her she should choose.

'You'll get fat,' observed her brother.

'I have to keep my strength up. Becky, sit here by me—isn't it lucky that we don't have to diet or anything dreary like that? I shall eat two cream cakes.'

Becky ate two as well while the Baron sat back drinking his tea and making do with a small slice of plain cake, entertaining them with light conversation the while.

They reached Molde in the early evening and the Baron slowed to idle through the little town so that Becky had time to look around her. And there was plenty to see. Molde lay on the north bank of a fjord with mountains towering behind it and the fjord before it, its calm water besprinkled with a great many islands and beyond them in the distance, the Molde Panorama—eighty-seven mountains, snow-capped, providing a magnificent backdrop to the charming little place. Becky, almost twisting her neck off in order to see everything, allowed her gaze to drop finally on to the street they were driving through; the main street, lined with shops and filled with people on holiday and ending presently at the quay side, where it changed abruptly into a pleasant road lined with villas. They didn't go as far as this, though. The Baron drew up opposite the quay, said 'Here we are,' and got out.

The hotel was modern and large, overlooking the fjord, and after the bright sunshine outside the foyer looked cool and welcoming. And the Baron was known there; they were taken at once to their rooms overlooking the loch, each with a balcony. Becky, after a quick look round the comfortable apartment, went straight outside. There was a ferry coming in and a good deal of bustle on the quay only a few hundred yards away, and coming up the fjord from the open sea was a liner, its paintwork gleaming in the evening sun. She rested her elbows on the balcony rail and watched its speedy approach until the Baron's voice, very close, interrupted her.

He was on the balcony next to hers, doing just as she was doing. 'Nice, isn't it?' he asked mildly. 'I've been here several times and I never tire of it. What shall we do first? Drinks and dinner and then a stroll? We can explore the town tomorrow.'

'But you must know it very well already?' said Becky practically.

'Oh, I do—but there's always a certain smug satisfaction in showing people around when you know it all and they don't.'

She laughed then and he said: 'You should laugh more often, Becky—there's no reason why you shouldn't now, you know.' He smiled at her and nodded. 'I'm going to have a shower and change. About half an hour suit you? Tialda takes ages . . .'

He went into his room and Becky stood where she was and didn't say a word. She should laugh more often, should she? Was he implying that she was dull and incapable of enjoying herself? What was it he had said? No beauty and no sparkle. She went inside herself. What did he suppose she had to laugh about, in heaven's name?

CHAPTER FOUR

THEY dined at a table in the window and as the restaurant overlooked the quay, they had a splendid view of the liner berthing for the night and its passengers streaming ashore. The little town was lighted now, although the mountains beyond the fjord still had their snow-capped summits gilded with the very last of the sun. It was a little paradise, thought Becky, sipping her sherry and staring out at it all. She turned when the Baron spoke; he was sitting opposite her, his elbows resting on the table, his hands clasped before him. He had nice hands, large and well-shaped and with well-kept nails; they looked, she decided, very dependable.

'Daydreaming?' he asked idly, and she went a little pink because she must have seemed rude, ignoring her companions.

'No, just a bit overcome with the scenery.'

He nodded. 'We'll go across to Hjertoya beach tomorrow—it's on that island straight ahead. You swim?'

She nodded. 'But I haven't got a swimsuit.'

'And I want a bathing cap,' declared Tialda. 'We'll go out early, Becky, and get them.' She picked up the menu. 'What shall we eat?'

The food was mouthwatering; Becky settled for crabmeat cocktail, chilled strawberry soup, Virginia ham with rum and raisin sauce with a salad on the side because the Baron assured her that that was essential to her good health, and by way of dessert blueberry pie with whipped cream. She and Tialda drank a delicious white wine, but the Baron took red wine with his tenderloin steak and brandy with his coffee. They went for a stroll afterwards; just along the main street, past the modern town hall and the whitewashed church above it.

'We'll go in there tomorrow,' promised the Baron. 'It was rebuilt after the Germans destroyed it during the war—it's beautiful.'

Becky wandered along in a pleasant dream. It was cool and she hadn't got a jacket with her because she hadn't got one; and who would dream of wearing a navy blue cardigan with the flowered shirt and the lacy blouse? And when the Baron wanted to know if she were warm enough she was quite emphatic about saying that she was, and if his mouth twitched a little at seeing her little shivers, she didn't see it.

They took a water taxi across the fjord to the bathing beach the next morning, and Becky had never been so happy. She was a good swimmer and the water was surprisingly warm. She forgot that her swimsuit was a cheap one-piece, its complete lack of glamour highlighted by Tialda's expensive beach outfit, she forgot that her future was precarious to say the least, she even forgot the amused glance the Baron had flung at her as she had waded into the water and struck out into the calm blue waters of the fjord; just for the present, life was everything she could wish for.

She tired presently and turned on to her back to rest, and found the Baron idling alongside her. 'Who taught you to swim?' he wanted to know.

'My father.' She remembered the look of amusement and turned over and began to swim back to the beach. 'I'll go and keep Tialda company,' she called as she passed him. But she couldn't escape him; he kept beside her without difficulty, so that they arrived at the beach together to find Tialda half asleep in the sun. 'Oh, good,' she greeted them, 'you're back— I'm dying for something long and cool to drink. Tiele, be a darling and find something,' and when he had gone: 'There's a café half way up the beach. Becky, what a wonderful swimmer you are.' She chuckled. 'You've surprised Tiele—I expect he thought you could only paddle like me.' She rolled over and smiled at Becky who had dropped on to the sand beside her. 'Gosh, I'm hungry! I hope Tiele buys something to eat as well.'

He had; they drank lemonade and munched delicious outsize buns, thick with currants and then had one more swim before taking the taxi back again for lunch. And in the afternoon they strolled through the town to the church, where Becky wandered off by herself to enjoy its whitewashed walls and small vivid stained glass windows and the big colourful cross behind the simple altar—quite different from the cathedral at Trondheim but in its way just as magnificent. She found the others outside presently, sitting on the wall of the terrace overlooking the town and the fjord with the mountains beyond. There were roses everywhere and their scent filled the still warm air, and Becky, sniffing appreciatively, said: 'Oh, I'd like to come back here—I always imagined Norway to be cold and grey, and it's not at all ...'

'It is in the winter, although this is one of the warmer spots, that's why the roses are so abundant—Molde is called the Town of the Roses, did you know that? Becky, do you want to do any shopping? Tialda wants some hand-painted woodwork, supposing we go and look for it now?'

And so the day passed pleasantly enough, and the day after it, and Becky made the most of every minute of them. Right at the back of her mind was the unhappy thought that the Baron was a little bored by it all; he was charming and thoughtful and patient, but every now and then she caught that faint look of amusement on his face when he looked at her. She was annoyed by it but sad too; she could just imagine what he thought of her: a dowdy girl who wore cheap clothes and didn't know how to make the best of herself—and she wasn't really like that, but after two years of no money, no make-up and nothing new to wear it was difficult to splash out, for always at the back of her mind was the fear that it wouldn't last; that she would find herself with no job and no money again, and he was so secure himself that he would never have known the insecurity that not having money brought with it.

They went back on the fourth day after a last lunch overlooking the quay and the lovely fjord, the boot filled with painted wooden knick-knacks which Tialda had taken a fancy to, and a great armful of roses which the Baron had bought just to prove, he pointed out, that they had been to Molde. And Becky had bought something too; a delicate glass vase to hold one rose; it had been expensive but she hadn't been able to find anything else, and besides, the Baroness seemed to have everything she could possibly want.

She found herself in the front seat beside the Baron when they left, to be entertained by him with a gently amusing conversation for the entire journey, and when, at the end of it, she tried to thank him for her holiday he just as gently ignored her, so that after one or two attempts she gave up, sensing his faint impatience with her.

'I'm glad you enjoyed it,' he observed carelessly. 'And now you face the herculean task of getting my mother organised to leave the day after tomorrow.'

Which somehow reduced her to the status of a wage-earner in his household. Which, after all, she was.

Indeed, she was kept so busy upon her return that she hardly saw him or Tialda during the next day. The Baron had friends to visit in Trondheim and took Tialda with him, and as he was out for dinner on the following day and was so late for lunch that she had it alone, by reason of Doctor Iversen's visit, she saw him only briefly. But they met unexpectedly only a few hours before they were to leave; the Baroness had told Becky to have an hour or two off while she enjoyed a last gossip with her sister, and Becky had seized the opportunity to go to the cathedral just once more. And there, standing quietly in a corner admiring its sombre magnificence, she had been joined by the Baron. He said nothing at all, only nodded, faintly smiling, and after an awkward moment or two she had given an abrupt nod in answer and walked away. But he had been at the door when she reached it and together they crossed the flagstones and went through the gate which led to the front of the cathedral.

'I hardly expected to find you here,' remarked the Baron.

It seemed that he intended to walk back with her. 'Why not?'

'I should have imagined that a last round of the shops would have been more to your liking.'

'Why?'

He stopped to look at her in surprise. 'Well, girls like shopping, don't they? Don't you?'

'I love it,' declared Becky promptly, 'but I can see shops in any town, but I can't see Trondheim Cathedral anywhere but here.' She walked on briskly, annoyed with herself because she had sounded like a prig and annoyed with her companion for not saying another word until they reached the house, when all he said was: 'We leave directly after lunch, so will you do the last-minute chores now? Someone will be up for the luggage in about ten minutes.'

She had whisked upstairs and in the teeth of the Baroness's complaints that she hadn't finished with her jewel case, beauty box, a selection of hats—one of which she still had to decide upon—and several pairs of shoes, she did as her employer had asked and then changed into uniform, rammed her hair under her cap in a very severe fashion, and trod downstairs to search for the handbag the Baroness had left somewhere but couldn't remember where, and when she met the Baron in the hall she gave him such a stern look that he opened his eyes very wide indeed. Tialda had seen the look as she came out of the sitting room and when Becky had gone back upstairs she slipped a hand into her brother's arm, grinning up at him.

'What does it feel like?' she wanted to know. 'You're—how old? thirty-eight—and ever since I can remember girls have fallen over themselves to get you interested. You've never bothered with any of them— well, not many, anyway, and here's Becky ...'

'I'm not interested in Becky either, Tialda.' The Baron's voice was soft and very gentle and his sister said hastily:

'I didn't say you were, so don't come the big brother over me.' She giggled: 'All the same, she'll make some man a very good wife one day; he'll have to put his slippers on in the house and exercise the dog and bring her tea in bed—oh, and of course she'll have children, very well behaved ones.'

The Baron frowned faintly, but his voice was light. 'Which is more than we can expect from your brats; you were a most unpleasant little girl.'

She beamed up at him. 'Wasn't I? But I'm nice now.' She reached up and gave him a sisterly peck on the cheek. 'There are an awful lot of nice girls around,' she wheedled. 'Surely there's one you fancy?'

'I fancy any number,' he told her blandly, 'but not to marry. Besides, I've no time for a wife—there is so much work ...'

'Pooh! You find time to take Nina van Doorn out —she only has to pout at you and roll those eyes. It would save a lot of time and trouble if you married her ...'

'Would you like that, Tialda?'

'No—I can't stand the girl, but that's natural, she outshines the lot of us with all that gorgeous hair, we none of us stand a chance. I wonder how Becky will feel when she sees her ...'

'Why Becky?'

'I don't suppose you've looked at her long enough to see that she's plain—nice eyes, but her face is too thin and pale, and she drags all that hair back ... Oh, well, I must go and throw the last few things in, I suppose.'

Tialda wandered off, leaving her brother staring at nothing and frowning again.

It said much for the Baron's powers of persuasion that the party left exactly at the time he had suggested. His mother, never very punctual and used to having her own way, had thought of a dozen things which had to be done at the last minute; friends she wanted to say goodbye to once more, even a letter to write, to all of which her son had a suitable answer, so that the Rolls, with Becky and her patient in the back, the luggage safely stowed and he driving with Tialda beside him, took the road south in the early afternoon sunshine.

Because of the Baroness's leg, still in plaster, and her dislike of long car journeys, they travelled only as far as Otta, about a hundred and fifty miles away, and here they put up for the night. The Baroness was inclined to be demanding in a charming way and already declaring that she ached all over, was giddy from looking at so many mountains and convinced that she would be unable to go on the next morning. Becky soothed her in a motherly fashion, put her to bed and saw to it that she had her dinner brought to her there, and then, because she was still a little querulous, suggested a game of cribbage. They were deeply immersed in this when the Baron and Tialda came to enquire why Becky hadn't gone down to dinner and it seemed sensible to relinquish her chair to the Baron and go with Tialda, who declared that she was quite able to eat her dinner for a second time if Becky wanted company.

And all the Baroness's discomforts had disappeared by morning. The Baron waited patiently while Becky helped her patient to ready herself for the day, stowed her into the car carefully, and set off once more. They had the whole day before them, which was a good thing since they had a great distance to go; Kristiansand was some three hundred and eighty miles distant and the roads, although good, were in many parts mountainous, but as the Baron pointed out, he had done the trip several times, he knew the road and provided they stopped frequently for his mother's benefit, he saw nothing out of the way in attempting such a long trip in country where half that distance was considered a fair day's driving. And he was right; there was little traffic as it was early for the tourists and the Baroness, kept amused by Becky, felt no discomfort. They stopped in Drammen for lunch and Brunkeberg for tea, and arrived at Kristiansand in good time to rest before a late dinner. And the following morning there was no hurry; they were to go on the midday ferry to Hirtshals, drive the hundred and fifty odd miles to Vejle and go on again in the morning.

Another three hundred and fifty miles; Becky doing sums on the back of an envelope was staggered at the amount of ground they were covering. Normally, she supposed that they would have all been bone-weary by now, but they stopped frequently and had nothing to do each evening but have their dinner and go to bed, although it wasn't quite as easy for her as all that, because her patient needed a good deal of attention at the end of the day and exercises had to be done, however unwilling the Baroness was to do them. But the Baron showed no signs of tiredness. He drove superbly and nothing appeared to disturb his calm. The journey had been well organised before they set out and he knew exactly when and where to stop, and although he took it for granted that Becky would have her hands full he was careful of her comfort. She wouldn't have missed their journey for all the tea in China. She was sorry that it was almost over and her job with it, as the Baroness was making steady progress; within a week of their return she would have the plaster off and exchange her crutches for a stick and then, Becky supposed, she wouldn't be needed any more.

That the Baron would find her a job she never doubted, but working in hospital might not be as pleasant as living in the lap of luxury with the Baroness. She consoled herself with the thought that she would have Bertie and Pooch again and it would be fun making a home for the three of them. She had no reason to complain, she told herself firmly, and concentrated upon seeing as much of Denmark as possible as they drove down from the ferry. It was entirely different from Norway and as on parts of the road at least there was no speed limit, she managed to get only brief glimpses of the country, but in the towns and villages where the Baron had to slow down, she had ample chance to look around her. Everything was very neat and clean and she admired the rolling farmland with beech woods and pine plantations dotted here and there, and she was charmed with Vejle although she saw very little of it. The Baroness was tired and cross and it took Becky a long time and a good deal of her patience to settle the little lady for the night. But she was her charming self in the morning, eager to start, for as she pointed out to Becky: 'We shall be home this evening, my dear. I know it's quite a journey, but Tiele has promised that I shall eat dinner under his roof tonight.'

'Isn't it your roof too?' asked Becky.

'No—I lived there while my husband was alive, but now I live in our town house in Leeuwarden— quite close, you know. But Tiele wishes me to spend the night at Huis Raukema.'

So they set off once more on the last lap of the journey; another three hundred and sixty miles, six hours' travelling, the Baron assured them, and frequent stops. 'For we have all day to kill,' he pointed out. 'It's not yet eleven o'clock and I told Willem to expect us in time for dinner.' He looked at Becky. 'Someone should have warned you that I enjoy driving. On my own I should have travelled much faster ...'

'I am enjoying the journey very much,' Becky told him sedately.

It was exciting to cross into Germany and then later, into Holland at last. The country looked rather like Denmark although the farms were larger with enormous barns at their backs and great herds of cows grazing in the flat water meadows. They bypassed Groningen and once clear of the city took a country road running north, side by side with a wide canal, but after a while the Baron turned off to the west, cutting across the flat countryside until they reached another canal bordered by trees. It was a peaceful landscape with small villages, each with its church dominating it and dykes encircling the low-lying land. Leeuwarden lay somewhere ahead, Becky supposed, but there was no sign of it at present. Perhaps this was a short cut ...

The Baron, who had been travelling fast along a familiar road, slowed the car presently and Becky, watching the canal slip past them, exclaimed with delight when she saw the narrow arm of water leading from it. It was lined with trees too and as well as that there were cottages along the water's edge, half hidden from the road and in the distance a church. 'Oh, that's really very pretty,' declared Becky to no one in particular.

'You like it? That's where we're going,' said the Baron. He kept on driving though and it was a minute or two before he turned into a narrow lane which led off the road towards the canal and the village on the other side of the water. They had to cross a bridge to reach it, a quaint affair which opened for boats and barges to pass; Becky was still looking back at it as they reached the first few cottages.

The village was small, peaceful and pretty, its church large enough to accommodate ten times the number of its inhabitants. The road wound past it and into a small wood fenced in, and after a minute or two the Baron turned the car for the last time into a sanded drive between thick shrubs and trees. 'Home,' said the Baroness softly.

Home, decided Becky, peering in front of her, was a place of splendour, standing proudly at the end of the drive; a large square house backed by a semicircle of trees—one of every species, she thought flippantly, gazing at their variety and lowering her gaze to take in the velvet lawns and the flower beds blazing with colour. The drive ended in a sweep and the Baron brought the Rolls to a gentle stop before the shallow steps leading to a massive porch and double doors, already opening. Becky got out, bent on making herself useful, and while Tialda ran excitedly up the steps she gathered the Baroness's bits and pieces and followed the Baron at a more sober pace. There was an elderly man at the door, but beyond a brief reply to his greeting, the Baron with his mother in his arms didn't pause on his way. He crossed the lofty wide hall, with Willem ahead of him to open one of the many doors leading from it, and strode through it with Becky on his heels, very wishful to stop and look around her but not daring to. Just inside the door he paused for a second, which did give her a chance to see that the room was large, beautifully furnished and despite that contrived to look cosy, but when she heard him speak she brought her gaze back to the broad shoulders in front of her.

'Nina!' said the Baron in a voice she hadn't heard before. 'I didn't expect you to be here.'

Becky heard a trill of laughter and skipped a couple of steps to one side so that she could see round the massive back before her. In the centre of the room stood a girl—a beautiful creature with golden hair brushed into the fashionable untidy mop, and exquisite features. She was wearing a dress of some soft material in palest blue with a full skirt and a tiny bodice which showed off her slenderness to perfection and she was smiling confidently across the room at the Baron.

'Is it a lovely surprise?' she wanted to know, quite sure that it was, and waited while he made his mother comfortable in one of the straight-backed armchairs by the open french window before crossing the room and lifting her face to his. Becky looked away as he bent his head to kiss her and wished that she wasn't there. This couldn't be his wife; he had never mentioned one—his fiancée, then ...

'Nina,' said the Baron formally, 'this is Miss Rebecca Saunders who is looking after Mama. Becky, Juffrouw Nina van Doorn.'

The girl murmured something in her own language and Becky's face went wooden because she guessed it was something about her, but then Juffrouw van Doorn smiled and said How do you do so pleasantly that she decided that she had been mistaken, but she had no opportunity to think about this as the Baron went on smoothly: 'Becky, will you go upstairs and make sure that my mother's room is quite ready for her? You'll find someone in the hall to take you up—I'll bring the Baroness up in ten minutes. She should have supper in bed, I think.'

Becky was only too glad to escape. Somehow it wasn't quite what she had expected, but of course after the carefree weeks with the Baroness, she had rather forgotten her position in the household. And she had wanted to go at once to see Bertie and Pooch.

She swallowed disappointment and went out of the room to where a nice-faced middle-aged woman was waiting.

'Sutske,' she said, and smiled, and Becky put out a hand.

'I'm the nurse,' she said, hopeful that she would be understood.

'Zuster Saunders,' nodded the housekeeper cheerfully, and beckoned her to follow.

The staircase was at the back of the hall, its graceful wings branching left and right to the gallery above. Sutske didn't hurry and Becky had time to look about her as they went, her head over one shoulder as they climbed. The hall was square, its crimson wall hangings divided by white-painted wall pillars picked out with gold, a circular window in the roof high above her head lighted it and the polished wood floor was spread with thin silk rugs. It looked very grand, and the gallery when they reached it was just as grand; the walls were all white here and in place of rugs there was a thick crimson carpet. Becky paused a second to look down into the hall before following the housekeeper to one end of the gallery where that lady opened a door and ushered her inside. This was to be the Baroness's room, then, a vast apartment with windows on two walls, a canopied bed, a number of very comfortable chairs, a marquetry tallboy and a graceful sofa table under one of the windows with a triple mirror upon it.

Left alone, Becky, in a panic that the Baroness would arrive before she was ready for her, turned back the bed, plumped up the pillows and went to see what was behind the three doors in the room. A bathroom, splendidly appointed in the same soft pinks and blues as the curtains and coverlet, an enormous clothes closet, in which she saw that the Baroness's things for the night were already disposed, and the last door, leading into a small lobby with another open door at its end. Another bedroom which would be hers, she surmised, much smaller but every bit as charming. She didn't waste time exploring further, but went to put out soap and sponge, her patient's night things, and lay her brushes and combs on the dressing table. And just in time, for the door was thrust open and the Baron walked in, carrying his mother.

He didn't speak to Becky, only nodded vaguely before he went again, and his mother said dryly: 'Now he can go back to Nina ...' She stopped and went on in quite a different voice: 'Dear Becky, you have everything ready—I'm a little tired. Tiele says something on a tray—he told Sutske to send it up in about an hour.'

Perhaps Becky was more tired than she knew, but the hour seemed very long, and indeed by the time the Baroness was sitting up in bed with a dainty supper on the bed table before her, she was as worn out as her patient and a good deal more hungry. and over and above that was the urge to go in search of Bertie and Pooch. No one had mentioned them yet, and with the beautiful Nina downstairs it was hardly likely that the Baron would remember them. After what seemed an age the Baroness was settled for the night and Becky, leaving one small lamp alight, went softly from the room with the tray.

It was very late, possibly everyone had gone to bed and although Tialda had been in to say goodnight some time ago, declaring that she was going to bed too and reminding Becky that there would be some supper for her downstairs, Becky had not the least idea where to go for it. If she found the kitchen there might be coffee, though, and at the same time she would have a quick look for Bertie and Pooch ... perhaps it wasn't quite the thing to prowl around the house in that fashion, but she felt that she had excuse enough; besides, she wasn't likely to meet anyone.

She met the Baron; he was coming in through the front door as she gained the last stair and since she could hear the whine of a receding car, she concluded that his visitor had just left. He frowned when he saw her and said: 'Good lord, are you still up?'

It would hardly be her ghost and she was tempted to say so. 'Yes,' she told him briefly, and made for the back of the hall where she had noticed a baize door.

'You don't have to carry trays in this house.' The Baron's voice had an edge to it.

'There's no one about,' she pointed out matter-of-factly.

'Then I'll ring for someone ...'

Becky quite forgot who he was. 'Indeed you won't,' she told him roundly. 'Getting people out of their beds at this hour—do you know how late it is?'

He didn't need to answer, for the great Friesian wall clock creaked into life and chimed midnight in a mellow old voice. 'You've had supper?' he asked carelessly as he turned away.

'No.'

He was beside her then, taking the tray from her.

'My dear girl, what a thoughtless man I am!'

'No, not really—Tialda came and told me that there would be supper downstairs for me; your mother was very tired—too tired to settle easily. She's asleep now.'

He stood looking down at her, the tray balanced on one hand. 'I'm afraid I have neglected you all. We will go to the kitchens now and see what we can find.'

Becky was suddenly cross as well as tired, nothing had been quite what she expected; the grandeur of the house and she had thought that at least someone would have mentioned Bertie and Pooch. 'Thank you,' she said snappily, 'I shall do very well—I'm not in the least hungry,' which was a lie, 'but I should like to know if Bertie and Pooch are all right, Baron.'

'Oh, God—that too! Forgive me, Becky. Of course they're all right—I'll take you to them now.'

He put a hand on her back and swept her along and through the baize door, down some steps and into a large kitchen, equipped to the last skewer and still somehow looking delightfully old-fashioned. There was an Aga stove along one wall and on the rug before it were Bertie, Pooch and a Great Dane. All three animals turned round, half asleep, and then bounded to their feet and rushed across the kitchen, the Great Dane to hurl herself at the Baron, Bertie and Pooch to cover Becky with joyful licks, pushing and shoving her in their efforts to greet her properly after such a long time. She sank on to the floor and let them have their way while the tears ran down her cheeks. They hadn't forgotten her, and very soon they could set up house somewhere and she wouldn't have to leave them again. She forgot her companion completely, but presently he bent down, plucked her to her feet, ignoring the tears and remarked cheerfully: 'There's coffee—it's always on the stove in case I have to go out at night—and I've found some rolls and butter and cheese and there's a salad in the fridge.'

He sat her down at the scrubbed wooden table in the middle of the kitchen and poured coffee for them both while the Great Dane trod quietly at his heels.

Becky drank some of the coffee, wiped her eyes and found her voice. 'Thank you very much, Baron, for taking such good care of them.' And at his noncommittal grunt: 'What do you call your dog?'

'Lola.'

'Why do you call her that?'

'What Lola wants, Lola gets,' quoted the Baron. 'She rules this place with a rod of iron, although she's as gentle as a lamb. Your two get on very well with her.' He buttered a roll and put some salad on a plate. 'And now eat your supper—such as it is.'

Becky ate, with Pooch on her lap and Bertie sitting as close to her as he could get, the Baron plying her with food and coffee while he carried on a conversation which really needed no reply from her, which gave her time to resume her usual composed manner. But presently she had had enough and began to pile the supper things tidily.

'Oh, leave that,' he spoke impatiently, 'someone will see to it in the morning.'

Becky went on collecting plates and cups and saucers. 'My stepmother and Basil did that—left things for the morning. You have no idea how beastly it is to come downstairs and find a lot of dirty crockery to wash up.'

'No, I haven't, and I can assure you that there are sufficient staff in my household to find the task bearable—and may I remind you, Becky, that this is my house and I do exactly what I wish in it, and I expect its other occupants to do as I ask.'

His self-assurance was a little daunting. She said uncertainly: 'Oh, you do?' and beyond gently laying the china in her hands on the tray, she stopped what she was doing. There was no point in annoying him; she seemed to do that easily enough anyway. She got up, wished Bertie and Pooch goodnight and directed them back to their rug, and went to the door where she turned to say: 'Goodnight, Baron.'

'Why do you persist in calling me Baron?' he asked testily.

'Well, you are,' she said reasonably. 'Thank you for my supper and for taking such good care of Bertie and Pooch.'

He had been sitting at the table but he reached the door at the same time as she did. 'Tiele, perhaps?' he asked persuasively.

'Certainly not—you're my employer, and it wouldn't be right.'

He shrugged his shoulders. 'Please yourself.'

He bent his head suddenly and kissed her as she passed him.

CHAPTER FIVE

THE Baroness was tired the next morning. Becky, leaving her propped up against the pillows, having her breakfast, went to find the Baron and tell him so. She had seen him earlier from the window, astride a great horse, returning from an early morning ride—he looked rather splendid on horseback, she conceded, wondering at the same time whether he worked the normal long hours of a doctor or held a part time post at some hospital. In any case, since he was a doctor, he could decide if his mother was fit to get up. Personally, Becky considered that the little lady had exhausted herself on their long journey and needed at least a day in bed, if not two. She found him in the small breakfast room, a small, panelled apartment at the side of the house, having been shown there by Willem, and as she went in, just for a moment she felt shy, remembering the previous evening, but only for a moment. His kiss hadn't meant a thing and it certainly couldn't have been because she had looked attractive, more the sort of comforting kiss one would give an old lady who had lost her purse ... She gave him a polite good morning and asked him, still very politely, if he could spare the time to see his mother. 'Before you go to work,' she explained, just to make it quite clear.

'Ah—bent on getting my nose to the grindstone again, are you? Well, I have two more days of my holiday, and when my mother is staying with me,' he added blandly, 'I visit her every morning after breakfast.'

Becky took no notice of the way he was looking down his high-bridged nose at her—very intimidating, but she wasn't going to be intimidated.

'I supposed that you would be going to work, Baron.'

'Then I suggest that you give up supposing and wait until you are told.'

She gritted her little white teeth and without answering him, walked out of the room. Two could be rude!

The Baroness wouldn't have finished her breakfast yet. Becky hadn't had hers either and she had no idea where to go for it—the kitchen, perhaps. There would be some sort of servants' hall, she supposed, and Tialda on the previous evening had told her that her supper was downstairs—besides, it was a splendid chance to see Bertie and Pooch.

Sutske was there with two young women and they all looked up and smiled as Becky went in. She smiled back and stood still while Bertie and Pooch made much of her, and since no one had said anything about breakfast she went through the open door at the back of the kitchen, into the yard at the back of the house. It was almost encircled with outbuildings, its cobbled surface uneven and worn by countless footsteps. Becky walked briskly to where an open archway led to the grounds beyond and was on the point of continuing down the back drive when the Baron popped up beside her, apparently coming from one of the great barnlike buildings on either side of her.

'You walked away,' he remarked mildly. 'I was on the point of asking if you would care to breakfast with me.'

She stood to answer him, Pooch under one arm, Bertie pressed to her side.

'Thank you, no. If you would tell me where I'm to have my meals ...?'

He lifted his eyebrows. 'My dear girl, with us, of course—where else?'

She eyed him stonily. 'I was waiting to be told,' she said sweetly.

He laughed then and caught her by the arm and turned her round to walk her back into the house. He called something to Sutske as they went through the kitchen and when they reached the breakfast room Willem was laying a place for her. Bertie and Pooch had come too and at the door Becky paused. 'Do you mind the animals?' she asked diffidently.

'Not in the least. Lola is under the table if you care to look.'

He drew out a chair for her and sat down himself. 'You're worried about my mother?'

'Not worried exactly; she's tired—it was a long journey and although she loved every minute of it, I think it exhausted her.'

'We'll keep her in bed for today, then, and tomorrow as well. If she's quite rested then, you can go back with her on the day after that.'

Becky buttered a roll and laid a wafer of cheese

on it, wondering if she could ask about Bertie and Pooch, but before she could frame a suitable request, the Baron spoke. 'You'll take the animals with you, of course. Lola will miss them—so shall I and the rest of us here. Will they be all right in a strange house until you leave my mother?'

'Oh, yes. They'll go wherever I do.' She hesitated. 'How do I get another job? The Baroness isn't going to need me for much longer, is she? Would you mind if I started looking for something before I leave?'

'You will remain with my mother for at least another week, perhaps longer, and I will see to it that you have somewhere to go, and work in one of the hospitals, either in Leeuwarden or Groningen.'

She blinked. He seemed very sure about it, but it was a relief to know that she wouldn't have to worry about that herself. She still had to make herself familiar with Holland and its ways, let alone the language, which sounded impossible at the moment. She thanked him and asked if Tialda was all right. 'She looked tired last night; if she wants to spend a day in bed I don't mind looking after her,' she offered.

'I looked in on her on my way down this morning; she's fine—plans to go shopping, I believe. She's going to stay here for a while. Pieter—her husband—will be back in another two weeks.' He was interrupted by the telephone and he got up to answer it and Becky got up too. As she did so she heard him say: 'Nina . . .' and although she couldn't have understood a word if she had remained, she swept Pooch up in her arms and with Bertie at her heels, left the room.

She didn't see him for the rest of that day. He had visited his mother, but she had left them together and when she returned he had merely left a message that his suggestions made at the breakfast table were to stand.

She didn't see him on the following day either; as she dressed that morning she had seen him ride away with Lola beside him and when he had gone up to visit the Baroness, Becky herself was eating a solitary breakfast with Willem to look after her and the animals for company. And since the family doctor came to see the Baroness just before lunch and stayed for a long time, there was no question of either Becky or her patient going to that meal. Doctor van Diessen was elderly, with a weatherbeaten face and twinkling blue eyes. He had known the family for so long that he was more of a friend than a doctor to them. He finished his examination of the Baroness although, as he observed, the legs were nothing to do with him—specialists would see to those very shortly. But he pronounced her very fit and agreed that there was no reason why she shouldn't return to her own home the next day if she wished. 'You have this excellent young lady to look after you, and Tiele to watch over you both.' He beamed at them both and went away to find Tiele, refusing an invitation to stay for lunch because he had more patients to see.

But the Baron didn't lunch alone. Becky, looking idly out of the Baroness's window, saw a Mercedes sweep up the drive and stop by the front door. Nina van Doorn got out, wearing slacks and a silk shirt which made Becky green with envy and before she had closed the car door the Baron was beside her.

Becky turned away. They were well suited, the pair of them, she told herself. The Baron might be kind and when he remembered, thoughtful of others, but he was too self-assured, naturally so, for he had far too much of the world's goods; and Nina seemed to have been cast in the same mould. And why are you worrying? Becky asked herself crossly. In another couple of weeks you'll never set eyes on them again.

The Baroness lunched in bed and Becky, summoned by the ever-attentive Willem, went downstairs presently and ate another solitary meal before settling her patient for a nap and going off duty for an hour or two. She changed into one of the cotton dresses she had bought in Trondheim and went to fetch Bertie and Pooch, and because she seemed to want to come too, Lola. The grounds round the house were parklike, and she left the formal gardens and wandered in the landscaped fields surrounding them, Pooch on his lead and the two dogs running free. They made for a little copse which bordered the boundary along one side and Becky, delighted to be free for a little while, didn't hurry. The sun was warm on her, her surroundings were idyllic and she had time to think.

But not for long. She had reached the copse and was wandering along one of its paths among the trees when she rounded a curve and saw the Baron and Nina van Doorn, deep in conversation, just ahead of her, Lola saw them too and launched herself at her master in a few great leaps, putting her paws on his shoulders to gaze into his face, and close behind her, not to be outdone, came Bertie, a good deal slower and much less agile and content to rub himself round the Baron's elegantly trousered legs. He didn't appear to mind in the least, although he told both beasts firmly to get down, but Nina minded very much. She had backed away, crying out something in a quite different voice from her usual cool tones, and when she saw Becky she began on her, remembering in her sudden rage to speak English.

'You!' she cried. 'You, with these animals—take them away at once, how dare you bring them here!' She rounded on the Baron. 'You know how I cannot bear them, they spoil my clothes.' Her voice soared. 'And don't dare laugh! Tell that girl to take them away—the servants should know better . . .'

The Baron's voice was soothing but amused. 'Don't be silly, Nina, they'll not harm you, and I think you have not recognised my mother's nurse. She is hardly to be blamed, she had no idea that you had such a dislike of dogs and cats.'

Becky had Bertie beside her again and Pooch tucked firmly under one arm. She said quietly: 'If Lola will come with me, I'll take her back with me. I'm sorry we disturbed you, Juffrouw van Doorn.'

Nina turned her back without answering and the Baron spoke quietly to Lola, who gave him a reproachful look, went to join Bertie and then followed Becky obediently back the way they had come.

It was a rather subdued little party that went back to the house. Becky had been shocked by the other girl's ill-temper and rudeness and the animals, sensing her feelings, had lost their enjoyment of a scamper. But it was much too soon to return to the house. Becky prowled round the gardens, seeking a quiet spot, and found one eventually; a rough patch at the

bottom of the walled kitchen garden, nicely hidden
by a row of raspberry canes and shaded by a mul-
berry tree. She settled on the grass, wound Pooch's
lead round her wrist, warned the dogs to behave
themselves and shut her eyes. Half an hour later,
while she was still in that strange world between
sleeping and waking, the dogs' sudden barking
brought her upright. The Baron was standing just inside the raspberry canes, looking down at her.

She stared back at him, her brown velvet eyes still
drowsy with sleep. 'Oh, lord,' she exclaimed crossly,
'can't we come here either?' She rubbed her eyes like
a sleepy child. 'How did you know we were here?'
She started to struggle to her feet, but the Baron put
out a large restraining hand and sat down beside her.

'It happens to be my hiding place. When I was a
small boy and had done something wrong—and that
was very often—I used to come here; for some reason
no one ever thought of looking behind the rasp-
berries. I come here even now with Lola.'

He stretched out his great length on the grass and
Lola lay down beside him. 'I'm sorry that Juffrouw
van Doorn was so upset. She had no intention of being rude—she simply didn't recognise you. She hates
most small animals ...'

Becky didn't speak. She was thinking that even if
she had been one of the servants she would have re-
sented Nina's tone of voice.

'She is a very beautiful girl,' went on the Baron,
choosing his words. 'I suppose that is why she cannot
bear to have a golden hair out of place or the tiniest
crease in her clothes.' His eyes fell to Becky's dress,
rumpled and creased where the dogs had lolled on

her. 'When a girl is as beautiful as Nina, she would not wish to spoil it in any way.'

Becky, for want of anything better to say, agreed politely, stroking Pooch's rather tatty fur as he lay curled in her lap.

'You're not envious of her?' enquired her companion softly.

'Me?' Becky thought about it. 'No, I don't think so. Of course it must be wonderful to know you're so lovely that everyone turns around to look at you and to know that all men are ready to eat out of your hand, but I wouldn't like it if I didn't like Pooch and Bertie and had to fuss about my clothes . . .'

'Juffrouw van Doorn hardly fusses,' remarked the Baron coldly, and Becky said hastily:

'Oh, I wasn't being personal. She's quite the most beautiful creature I've ever seen. You must think you're the luckiest man alive.'

'Oh? Why?' His silky voice should have warned her.

'Well, you're going to marry her . . .' She looked up and caught his icy stare. 'Well, it's none of my business,' she mumbled, going red.

'No, it isn't.' He had sat up, leaning his back against the tree, his casual friendliness all gone. 'This seems a good opportunity to discuss my mother and your future. She will return to her own home tomorrow and you with her, of course. I have arranged for her to be seen two days later; the plaster will be removed and if everything is satisfactory, she should be able to manage very well with a stick. I should be obliged if you will stay with her for a further week, during which time I will see about a job for you and

find you somewhere to live. Have you any prefer-
ence—surgical or medical?'

The red in Becky's cheeks had faded and she
looked quite pale again despite her days in the sun. It
was like accepting charity and it stuck in her throat;
he was carrying out his promise because he had said
that he would help her and he wouldn't go back on
his word. Charity could be very cold.

She said at once, her pleasant voice without expression, 'I like medical work, thank you, but I'll take
whatever there is going.'

He nodded and got to his feet. 'No, don't get up—
bring Lola in when you come, will you? I'll see what
there is and my secretary will let you know.'

Becky watched him go unhurriedly towards his
house. It was a pity, she reflected, that he was so
taken with Nina. She wouldn't be any good for him;
they both liked their own way far too well—though
perhaps if he loved her very much, he would let her
do exactly as she wanted. Becky scowled at the
thought—no dogs, no cats, certainly no horses or
donkeys, probably no children; sticky fingers would
anger Nina just as much as muddy paws. Becky
swept her still too thin arms round the necks of her
astonished companions and gave them a throttling
hug. Poor Lola, poor kitchen cats; she hoped the
Baron would find a kind home for them.

She saw very little of him for the rest of that day
and on the following afternoon, after a hectic morning persuading the Baroness to pack the few things
she had needed while she was staying with her son,
collecting Bertie and Pooch, putting her own small
possessions in her case, they drove away in an elderly

Cadillac, driven by an equally elderly chauffeur; both of them candidates for a museum, thought Becky, skipping into the front seat while Bertie, on his best behaviour, sat on the floor at the Baroness's feet. The Baron saw them off, Lola beside him, and his mother, reclining rather awkwardly in the back of the car, remarked comfortably: 'Of course, it's ridiculous to say goodbye. We live so close to each other and in any case he comes to see me frequently on his way to and from the hospital.'

Becky plucked up the courage to ask exactly what the Baron did.

'My dear child, has no one told you? Chests and hearts, my dear, just as his father before him. He has beds in Leeuwarden and Groningen and he goes frequently to London and Edinburgh and Birmingham —for consultations, you know. He works too hard, and it seems a pity that he should waste so much of his free time with someone as unsuitable as Nina van Doorn.'

To which bit of outspokenness Becky replied with a murmur. It was nice to think that someone else shared her views, though.

The Baroness lived in the centre of Leeuwarden in a beautiful old house in a quiet street lined with equally beautiful houses. Its door was opened by a slightly younger Willem, who Becky quickly learned was indeed that old man's brother, and he passed them carefully on to a severe and very tall woman rejoicing in the name of Jikke, who instantly took charge of the Baroness while at the same time welcoming Becky with an unexpectedly sweet smile and a complete lack of surprise at the sight of Bertie and

Pooch. Becky beamed back at her, happily unaware
that the Baron had made sure that his mother's
household would accept the two animals in an
amiable manner.

The party entered the house through an imposing
lobby which in turn led to a narrow hall, stretching
endlessly back to a gracefully curved staircase at its
end, and lined on both sides with doors. With Jikke
leading the way, Pooch under one arm and the
Baroness on the other, Becky slowly walked half its
length before the housekeeper opened a pair of doors
and ushered them into a small panelled room, very
cool and dim by reason of it having only one small
leaded window. Its floor was of polished wood with a
handsome rug before an old-fashioned and elaborate
stove, and several high-backed armchairs arranged
casually, interspersed by small tables holding charming lamps. There were bookshelves too and high on a
shelf above the panelling, rows of Delft plates and
dishes. It looked as though no one had touched it
since it was first furnished, centuries ago, thought
Becky, bidding Bertie sit while she set Pooch carefully beside him.

The Baroness smiled at her. 'We'll have tea before
we do another thing,' she declared, for all the world
as though she would be doing the unpacking and putting away of her many possessions, 'and then I shall
have my exercises before dinner. I've not asked anyone for this evening—indeed, I shall not do so until
this wretched plaster is taken off. I daresay we can
amuse ourselves for two days, Becky.' She allowed
Becky to make her more comfortable in her chair and
arrange the offending limb just so before saying:

'Ring the bell, will you? Ulco speaks English and he will tell you where your pets may sleep. You had better go with him when he comes.'

Which Becky did, through the hall again and a narrow wooden door, thick enough to withstand a siege, down a pair of steps and into a semi-basement kitchen, a nice old-fashioned place, fitted out cunningly with every modern device. It had a number of doors leading from it, and one of them revealed a roomy cupboard with a dog basket, comfortably blanketed.

'We thought that this is good, Zuster—if your dog and cat will sleep here—with an open door and you to lay them down before bed. We will not disturb them in the morning, but you will take them into the garden at the back?'

'Oh, splendid,' agreed Becky. 'I'll be down early, if no one minds?'

Ulco smiled at her. 'No one will mind, Zuster, and we take good care of them.'

She was really a lucky girl, mused Becky, as she sped back to the Baroness. Wherever would she have found someone who didn't object to animals, let alone went out of their way to accommodate them?

They had their tea, she and her patient, and then Becky left her patient to be taken upstairs where a cheerful young girl was already unpacking the Baroness's luggage in a vast room with an elaborate plastered ceiling and William and Mary walnut furniture. The curtains were a dusky pink and matched the bedspread and the white carpet was soft underfoot. Becky gave a willing hand in the disposing of her patient's wardrobe, smoothing silk and lace with a careful hand, loving the feel of it, and presently when they were finished the girl beckoned her to follow her through a door leading from the room which led directly into another bedroom. It was large too, simply furnished with white-painted bed, dressing table and tall chest, but it too had a thick carpet and easy chairs and enchanting little bedside lamps. The curtains were the same pink as in the Baroness's room and the bedspread was quilted rose-patterned chintz. There were books on the table by the bed too; Becky heaved a sigh of pure happiness and set about unpacking her own few garments.

It seemed very quiet after the Baron's great house and Becky found herself listening for his firm footstep around the place and his voice, never loud but clear and decisive. She was surprised at her pleasure when he arrived the following evening, walking in on the pair of them, the Baroness sitting in her lovely drawing room, stitching at her petit-point while Becky patiently unravelled silks for her.

'How very domestic,' was his comment as he joined them, and when Becky got up to leave them together: 'No, stay for a while, please—this concerns you, Becky.' He eased himself into a great armchair and stretched out his legs before him. 'Mama, I have arranged for you to be seen tomorrow afternoon at two o'clock. At the hospital—it will be easier there, as they will need the plaster shears to take that off your leg. You'll be seen in the orthopaedic consulting room and de Vries will make quite sure that everything is exactly as it should be. You will have to be X-rayed, of course, but there will be no waiting around. I shall be there for part of the time, but I have to be in Groningen in the morning, so don't expect me too early, will you.' He turned to look at Becky. 'You heard all that, Becky, is there anything else you want to know?'

'No, thank you, Baron.'

'I shall be obliged if you refrain from calling me Baron at the hospital—I prefer to be called Doctor.'

'Just as you wish, Doctor.' She sounded very meek.

'I sometimes suspect that you are laughing at me,' he observed blandly. And when she didn't answer: 'I should like to talk to my mother alone, if you wouldn't mind ...'

Becky skipped off to the kitchen where Pooch and Bertie had taken up residence as though they had lived there all their lives, and carried them off for a run in the narrow garden. It was a pleasant place, shaded by trees and bright with flowers and with a swing, long since forgotten, in one corner behind a hornbeam hedge. Becky sat herself on it with Pooch held firmly on her lap and idled to and fro in the sun. The swing squeaked each time she sent it back and forth; a pleasant sound, mingling with the birds around her and the chiming clocks in the city. She closed her eyes and allowed her thoughts to wander. She had some money saved now; once she had somewhere to live and a job she would buy some clothes. She began to reckon how long it would take her to save enough to buy a real silk shirt just like the one Nina van Doorn had been wearing ...

'Good lord,' said the Baron behind her, 'that swing hasn't been used since Tialda was a little girl and screamed her head off if I wouldn't push her. Do you want to be pushed?'

'No, thank you—Pooch is on my lap, I don't think he would like it.' She got out of the swing. 'I'll go back to the Baroness.'

'Do you get your free time, Becky?'

'Oh, rather,' she lied briskly without looking at him. 'Leeuwarden is just the kind of place I would choose to live in ...'

'That is fortunate,' his voice was bland, 'since it is to be your home. Jikke has a sister living on the other side of the city; she has an old house, converted into flats—I'm told that the top one is empty and she would be prepared to let you have it. She has no objections to animals provided they behave themselves. I will take you to see it tomorrow evening. This evening is impossible, I'm afraid, as I have an engagement.'

Nina, said Becky soundlessly to herself, and aloud: 'That's very kind of you, Doctor, but if you give me the address I'm sure I can find it on my own.'

'I have no doubt of that, but Mevrouw Botte speaks no English and you, I imagine, speak very little Dutch.'

'I have a dictionary,' said Becky with dignity, 'and I'm learning as fast as I can.'

'Yes, well—I doubt if you can learn sufficient to bargain with Mevrouw Botte by tomorrow evening. I'll call for you at half past six—I have already spoken to my mother.'

There was precious little time to think about it. By tea time the next day Becky was tired and irritable, although she hid that successfully from the Baroness. That little lady had been at her most trying; because she had been unable to decide what she should wear, they had very nearly been late for the appointment at the hospital and there had been a further delay when they reached it because she recalled suddenly that Willem's sister was in one of the wards, and she desired to see that lady first. It took tact and patience on Becky's part to explain to her that time to a consultant was precious, especially when he had made a special journey to see her—not to mention the houseman in attendance and a nurse or two.

In the end the plaster had been successfully removed, Becky had escorted her patient to X-Ray and then delivered her into the hands of Professor de Vries again. The examination had taken a long time, for he and the Baroness were very old friends and spent a good deal of time reminiscing about their youth. It wasn't until the Baron joined them that they got down to business, and Becky, asked to relieve the hospital nurse while she went to her tea and quite worn out with holding up X-rays, taking scribbled notes from the professor to various people whose whereabouts she had the greatest difficulty in finding in the vast and splendid new building, and supporting her patient when she was required to take a few steps, as well as fetching glasses of water, a fan because it was too hot, retrieving a mislaid handbag and encouraging her patient each time she declared that she was tired to death and couldn't they continue on the following day, could have fallen on his neck with relief. Not that she would have dared do any such thing. Somehow on his home ground, as it were, he looked unapproachable; older and remote, very much the consultant. He didn't notice her anyway; she doubted if he knew that she was there; she did as she

was told and when they had finally finished, put the
Baroness to rights once more, got her stick and
waited patiently to see what would happen next.

The Baron had escorted them out to the car, a
firm arm under his mother's, with Becky trotting behind, making sure that the Baroness used her stick
and didn't just wave it about as she was prone to do.
They had a small posse of people hovering behind
them; Out-Patients Sister, the Orthopaedic Registrar
and houseman, a couple of nurses and a porter in
case he was needed. The Baroness thanked them all
graciously, was settled in her car by the Baron and
with a thankful Becky beside her, had been borne
home once more.

And now Becky was free to get ready for her evening. The Baroness had a friend to see her and was
quite content to let her go directly after they had had
tea. Becky went up to her room after she had taken
Bertie and Pooch for a quick walk, and surveyed her
scant wardrobe. It would have to be the green jersey.
It had been a warm day, but the evening was overcast
and cooler. She got ready slowly and then had to
hurry over her face and hair because it was almost
half past six and she fancied that the Baron didn't
like being kept waiting. Probably he waited hours for
Nina, she thought as she sped downstairs and into the
hall.

He came out of the drawing room as she reached it,
wished her good evening and with a sidelong glance
at the green dress, suggested that they should waste
no time, but he stopped as they reached the door
where Ulco was hovering. 'I feel that Bertie and
Pooch should be with us. Wait here.'

He was back very quickly, with Pooch's battered head sticking out from under an arm, and Bertie walking sedately beside him. 'Lola's already in the car,' he told her.

Mevrouw Botte's house was ten minutes' drive away, in the centre of a narrow street of similar houses, all of them facing a canal with a line of trees and a wall beyond. It was quiet and had the advantage of being within fifteen minutes' walk from the hospital, and as Becky got out of the car she knew at once that she could be happy living in it. It remained to see if she felt the same way about Mevrouw Botte.

She did. That lady was at the door waiting for them, a small, bustling woman dressed in sober black, her hair strained back into a tidy knob from a round face whose most striking feature was a pair of boot-button eyes.

The Baron ushered his party into the narrow hall, introduced everyone, exchanged a few remarks with Mevrouw Botte and then stood aside to allow Becky to follow her up the steep narrow staircase.

There was a small landing on the first floor, with two doors, and on the second floor the landing was still smaller, so that the two doors were very close together, but the third landing was so minute it afforded nothing more than a foothold in front of its one door which Mevrouw now opened with a flourish.

The room within was surprisingly large, for it ran from the back to the front of the house, with a window at one end, and a door at the other. It was simply furnished with a disguised bed along one wall, a small round table with two chairs, a rather shabby easy chair, a little desk and a mirror over it. There were two doors side by side along the inner wall. One opened on to a cupboard of a kitchen, very neat and spotlessly clean, the other revealed a minute shower room. Becky beamed round her with delight; here was home at last.

'How much?' she asked breathlessly. 'Shall I be able to afford it?'

'Er—I'll ask Mevrouw Botte.' He said something to her which caused her black eyes to snap with amusement as she answered him, and then turned to Becky. The sum he mentioned seemed a great deal to her, but he added: 'You will earn three times as much as that each week. Would you be able to manage, do you think?'

'Oh, yes, I know I can. Does she really not mind Bertie and Pooch?'

The Baron smiled. 'Not in the least—you will see that there is a very small balcony outside the door and she will provide a large box in which they can sleep.' He glanced around him. 'It will be rather warm here, I fancy, and in the winter you will have to have some kind of heating. You wish to take it?'

'Yes, please. Would she like a week's rent in advance?'

'I imagine so—I believe that is the usual custom. You will be coming—let me see—a week today. Do you want her to do anything for you? Milk isn't delivered and nor is bread, but there are one or two shops close by.'

'Washing,' said Becky suddenly, and went to look at the balcony; very small with a high wall and a clothes line already stretched across it. There was room for the animals to sit there too—she would be able to go to work and leave the door open. The wall was too high for them to climb over; besides, they were both too elderly to entertain any such idea.

She went back to where the Baron and Mevrouw Botte were talking quietly together and got out her purse. 'And she will call each week for the rent,' explained the Baron. 'You feel you can cope with the language?'

Becky nodded. 'Oh, yes. I'll learn—I have to, you see.'

They bade Mervouw Botte goodbye and trailed down the stairs again and out to the car. On the way back the Baron told her that he had made an appointment to see the Directrice of the hospital on the following afternoon. 'A medical ward,' he explained. 'Women's, day duty, although you will have to do your share of night duty later on. You will be given Dutch lessons, although you will find that most of the staff speak English more or less.' He told her her salary too; it sounded a lot of guldens; probably she would be able to save quite a lot and buy some clothes. She became lost in a daydream for which she was roused by the Baron's impatient voice begging her to pay attention. 'For I am a busy man,' he reminded her, 'with no time to tell you everything twice.'

Becky said she was sorry in a meek voice and concentrated on all the do's and don'ts he was detailing for her benefit, and when they drew up before the Baroness's house once more she started to thank him. But she was barely halfway through her little speech when he cut her short quite curtly.

'My dear girl, don't make such a thing about it.'

He glanced at his watch. 'I'm already late for an appointment ...'

Becky had whipped out of the car, opened the door for Bertie and with Pooch over her arm poked her head back through the window.

'With Juffrouw van Doorn? If I'd known, Baron—Doctor—and what does it matter anyway?—I wouldn't have wasted your time. Still, I daresay you'll enjoy the rest of the evening all the more,' she added obscurely.

Her eyes were huge in her small face and dark with sudden temper. She withdrew her head before he could say anything and crossed the pavement and rang the door bell, wishing very much to have a good cry although she wasn't exactly sure why. Ulco's solemn kindly presence prevented her, though.

CHAPTER SIX

THE week flew by. The Baroness, while delighted that Becky had a job and somewhere to live, was a little peevish at the idea of her leaving. True, she had an abundant staff only too happy to fulfil her every whim, as Becky pointed out to her, but that proved to be no argument with her patient. 'I liked you the moment I set eyes on you, my dear,' declared the Baroness, 'and I am going to miss you. You will, of course, visit me whenever possible.'

And Becky, used by now to the little lady's imperious ways, said that yes, of course she would. 'I'm only a short walk away,' she pointed out, 'and I shall get off duty like everyone else.'

She had gone for an interview at the hospital, feeling scared, not because she wasn't sure if she could manage the job—she was sure of that, but worried that her tiny smattering of Dutch might decide the authorities against her. It was a tremendous relief to find that everyone, from the Directrice to the Home Warden who showed her over the Nurses' Home and where she could change each day, spoke English. She would have lessons in Dutch starting on the very first day and she would be expected to work hard at them and speak Dutch whenever possible. To start with, the Directrice explained, she would do routine work on the ward with another nurse until she felt that she was able to deal with patients on her own. 'And that shouldn't be long,' declared the Directrice cheerfully. 'It is amazing how quickly one learns if one applies one's mind to it.'

Becky had gone back to the Baroness's house with a dictionary and a book of Dutch medical terms, which she was delighted to find weren't so very different from the English ones—indeed, several of them were English. She had seen the Baron on the way, driving along the narrow street in his beautiful car. If he had seen her he gave no sign and she really hadn't expected him to; she had been rude and he must think her wretchedly ungrateful. Although she had tried to thank him ...

She had met the beautiful Nina too. She had gone into the city to do a small errand for the Baroness and coming out of the shop she had come face to face with Nina. She had smiled and said Hullo and been cut dead for her pains. But Nina had recognised her; her blue eyes had slid from Becky's tidy, mousey hair, down her cheap cotton dress, and come to rest on the sandals she had bought at Bata's.

And when, on her last day as the Baroness's nurse, she was about to leave for her new home, Nina and the Baron arrived together as she was waiting in the hall for the taxi, she remembered that look and her small determined chin went up. Nina nodded casually as she passed her, but the Baron stopped.

'Ah, yes, of course you start your new job tomorrow,' he remarked. 'Is everything O.K.?'

'Yes, thank you.' Becky gave him the briefest of glances and bent to adjust Bertie's collar.

'You're waiting for the car?'

Ulco answered for her, speaking in Dutch, and the Baron's reply sounded vexed. 'There is no need for you to have a taxi. I'll drive you over to Mevrouw Botte's house now.' He frowned down at Becky. 'There has been some misunderstanding.'

'No, there hasn't,' Becky told him, aware that Nina had paused on her way to the drawing room and was listening. She came back to them now and put a lovely useless hand on the Baron's arm. 'Tiele, don't hinder Nurse—you heard her say that she was waiting for a taxi. Your mother is expecting us ...'

The Baron's mouth could look exactly like a steel trap. He said quietly: 'Will you tell Mother, Nina? I shan't be more than ten minutes or so.' And then to Becky: 'I must apologise, Becky, it was not intended that you should leave like this.' He picked up her bag and nodded to Ulco, an interested spectator, to carry her case outside, and when she would have protested, took her arm, pausing only long enough at the door for Ulco to wish her goodbye.

'My mother has said goodbye to you?' he wanted to know as he opened the car door and ushered Bertie in.

'Yes, thank you.' Becky remembered that lady's tearful farewell and smiled faintly. The Baroness had been in no state to order the car or ask Becky how she was going to get to her new home; she had pressed a small flat parcel into Becky's hands and kissed her and then burst into tears. If it hadn't been for the faithful Jikke, Becky wouldn't have got away.

The short journey was accomplished in silence, with Becky sitting very upright with Pooch tucked firmly under her arm. At Mevrouw Botte's front door the Baron got out, fished out Bertie and went to hammer on the knocker before he went to help Becky, hampered by a rather restless Pooch, out. 'Upstairs with you,' he commanded, 'leave your bags, I'll bring them up.'

So Becky, with Bertie trailing behind her and Pooch craning his neck to see his new surroundings, went up the stairs behind Mevrouw Botte and on the top landing, received her key and was ushered into her very own flat.

It was, if anything, cleaner and neater than on her previous visit and on the table was a vase of summer flowers with a card tied to it. It read simply: 'Welcome to your home, Becky,' and she was bending to admire the bouquet when the Baron walked in with her things.

'Aren't they lovely?' She turned an excited face to him, quite forgetting that they had had little to say to each other. 'Whoever could have put them there? Would it be Mevrouw Botte?' She frowned. 'But she doesn't know that my name's Becky, and I'm sure it's not the Baroness ...'

'Why are you sure?'

She went pink. 'Well—she has no reason to do so.' She went on, making it brief: 'Thank you for bringing me, although it was quite unnecessary.'

He smiled faintly. 'Have you enough money, Becky? My mother remembered to pay you before you left?'

The pink deepened. 'I've quite enough money, thank you.'

'But you haven't been paid.' He smiled again. 'My mother never remembers anything.' He took a note case from his pocket and counted out notes and laid them on the table. 'If ever you need help or money, I hope you will ask me, Becky.'

It was the last thing she would ever do! If she hadn't needed the money she would have given it back to him with the greatest of pleasure; it only served to highlight the gulf between them. She gave a little gasp when he said softly: 'I get paid too, Becky —you don't have to look like that.'

He went to the door. 'I shall see you from time to time at the hospital, I daresay. I hope that you will enjoy your work and be happy here.'

She said thank you in a quiet little voice; he might dislike her and find her a nuisance, but he was the last link between her and the sheltered life she had been leading for the past month. She had a ridiculous urge to ask him to stay—just for a little while—while she got used to the idea of being on her own, but she had hindered him long enough; he would want to dash back to his Nina. He waited by the door for a moment as though he expected her to say more than that, and when she didn't speak he went away.

But there was too much to do for her to be lonely for long. Mevrouw Botte had stocked her cupboard with milk and enough food to feed them that evening and the following morning; she looked it over with satisfaction before unpacking her case, arranging the animals' box to their satisfaction and then, because it

was still a warm light evening, introducing them to
the balcony. It was quite late by the time they had
had their suppers and tidied up, and she had turned
the bed into a bed again and gone as silently as possible down the stairs with them both to take a walk
in the nearby small park.

It was a far cry from the luxurious bedroom she
had been sleeping in, but it was an even further cry
from her unhappy life in her stepmother's house.
Becky curled up in her narrow bed and slept, though
not before stifling a pang of regret for the pleasant
life she had been leading. 'At least I know now how
the other half lives,' she told herself, and Bertie and
Pooch, disturbed by her voice, muttered back at her.

She was on duty at half past seven in the morning,
which meant getting up at six o'clock, taking Bertie
and Pooch for their walk, having a quick breakfast
and walking to the hospital, but she would be home
before four o'clock, with the whole evening to call
her own. She skipped along the narrow pavement in
the fresh bright morning, eager to start but a little
nervous too.

But she need not have been; she had barely had
time to change into her white uniform dress and tuck
her hair under the plain white cap before a big girl
with very fair hair and blue eyes shot into the cloak-
room where the living out nurses changed and begged
her, in English, to go with her. The hospital was light
and airy and modern. Becky, who had trained in a
hospital which was a veritable nest of small passages
and endless staircases, found herself whisked into a
lift and borne upwards to a wide corridor lined with
closed doors. 'Administration,' breathed her guide,

and added in a friendly voice: 'My name is Riet—Riet van Blom.' She paused to hold out a hand which Becky shook.

'I'm Rebecca Saunders—Becky everyone calls me.'

They smiled at each other as Riet stopped before a door and knocked on it. Before she sped away she said hurriedly: 'I see you at coffee. I work also on the medical wards.'

Becky turned the handle and walked in. The Directrice sitting behind the desk in the severely furnished office was elderly, small and very round, with a severe hairstyle which made no attempt to keep up with fashion and very bright blue eyes. She wished Becky good morning and bade her sit before refreshing her memory from the papers before her.

'Doctor Raukema gives you a good reference,' she observed, 'and it is upon this I offer you the post of diploma'd nurse on the medical wards. You already know your salary; I told you during your first interview, and your working hours will be told to you by the Hoofd Zuster of your ward. Your Dutch lessons will commence immediately—they will be given during your duty hours, but you will be expected to study during your free time as well. If at the end of a month you are unable to reach the not very high standard we have set, then I am afraid we shall no longer be able to employ you.' She smiled suddenly. 'But I think there is little likelihood of that.' She rang a little bell and a door opened to reveal an elderly woman in a dark blue uniform. 'Juffrouw Markela will take you to your ward. I hope that you will be very happy with us.'

Becky murmured suitably and followed Juffrouw Markela from the office, glad that one hurdle had been crossed. It proved to be the first of many that morning, though; the wards looked the same; small six-bedded rooms leading off from a central area where the nurses' station stood, but there were any number of them and it was difficult at first to distinguish one from the other. All the doors looked alike, and so did the patients lying in their beds. Becky, flying rapidly behind Riet, discovered after the first panic that it was rather like the hospital had been at Leeds. The six ladies in the first ward she went into were all suffering from chest infections and it really didn't matter what it might be called in Dutch, the condition was exactly the same as she had nursed countless times in England, so that it didn't matter so very much that she could understand only one word in twenty or so; the routine was the same.

It was the same in all the wards and after a little while she began to gain some confidence, especially as some of the patients could speak a little English. And during the coffee break, she went downstairs with the cheerful Riet and met several more nurses, all of whom seemed prepared to accept her as one of themselves. She went back, much heartened by their friendliness, to plunge into the round of treatments, the giving of medicines and the making of beds.

She was going down to her dinner with two other nurses when she saw the Baron coming up the stairs they were going down. He was accompanied by his registrar, several housemen, a clerk bearing an armful of notes and a fierce-looking lady whom Becky took to be the social worker. She stood a little on one side to allow the party to pass her on the stairs and the Baron glanced at her briefly, accorded her the slightest of smiles as he drew level and continued on his way. Becky stared after him; she hadn't really expected him to stop, but she had hoped that he might.

She was tired when she reached her little flat that afternoon, but she forgot that in the delight of seeing Bertie and Pooch, sitting contentedly on the balcony, obviously nicely settled in. They all had tea and then she changed into a cotton dress and took them both for a walk in the park. It was cooler now and everyone was hurrying home from work. Becky climbed the stairs once more and once in her flat found herself wishing that she had a radio to break the quiet. But she didn't need one, she reminded herself. She had her Dutch lessons to study; she had had her first lesson that afternoon and it was all-important that she should learn that language as quickly as possible. She took a chair on to the balcony and with the animals sprawled at her feet, spent the next hour or so with her head in her books.

The next day was easier. She was on duty at ten o'clock until six in the evening, which meant that she could take Bertie and Pooch for their airing before going to the local shops for her food. It was a long time to leave her pets alone, although they had often had to spend whole days hidden away when Basil was in one of his tempers and Becky hadn't thought it safe for them to be at large, at his mercy. She fed them, tidied her little home and walked to work. And when she got off duty that evening she was too tired to do more than the usual walk in the park, make herself tea and toast, and go to bed early.

And the next day she was tired too, for she had late duty; from one o'clock until eight in the evening, but she was getting into the swing of the work now and it was easier, and Sister Tutor had been pleased with her progress with her Dutch lessons. She went to bed well content and lay for a little while going over her day.

She had seen the Baron again, for old Mevrouw Fiske, a heart patient, had had a mild coronary during the afternoon and the houseman, hastily summoned with the panic team, had been preceded by Doctor Raukema. It was Becky who had seen the old lady's sudden collapse, pressed the panic bell, flung the pillows to the ground, and with the patient flat on the bed, begun cardiac massage. By rights the patient should have been laid on the floor, but that was beyond her strength, and someone else should have been administering oxygen. Becky, working away at manual compression, sixty times a minute, had no time to worry about anything else. The panic bell should bring help within seconds, and it did—the panic team, running from their various duties, the houseman on duty, who had just left the floor and had further than anyone else to run, and the Baron, who happened to be passing the ward when Becky pressed the bell. Well ahead of everyone else, he had the patient on the floor and had taken over from Becky with a brief order for her to start mouth-to-mouth resuscitation before the team and its trolley arrived. The anaesthetist took over from Becky then and at a kindly nod of dismissal from Hoofd Zuster Witma, she slipped away, back to the six-bedded

ward on the other side of the corridor where she had
been going in the first place. It had been sheer luck
that she had happened to peer into Mevrouw Fiske's
room as she went past ...

She was arranging Juffrouw Drummel in her chair,
preparatory to making that lady's bed before the
three o'clock cup of tea came round for the patients,
when the half-open door was thrust open and the
Baron walked in. He wished the six inmates a pleasant good day and then crossed the ward to where
Becky was making the bed.

'Mevrouw Fiske has recovered,' he told her, watching her mitre a corner very neatly.

Becky straightened up. 'I'm very glad, sir—thank
you for coming to tell me.' She was still holding the
blanket, ready to turn it down neatly.

He frowned at her. 'Naturally I would tell you;
your prompt action undoubtedly saved her life.' He
turned on his heel, wished the patients goodbye with
great courtesy and went away. 'For all the world as
though I were to blame for the whole thing!' muttered Becky darkly, giving the pillows a tremendous
pummelling.

Before she slept she cried a little, although she had
no idea why.

She was on duty at ten o'clock the next morning.
She was beginning to get into the routine now and it
was astonishing how many words she had picked up,
mispronounced for the most part and heavily frowned
upon by Sister Tutor if she uttered them during her
lesson period, but she no longer felt so foreign, and
the nurses were friendly too and the registrar had

stopped and asked her how she was getting on. With Bertie and Pooch nicely settled for the day, she sped to work.

She hurried home just as quickly that evening. It had seemed a long day and a hot one, but now the evening was a little cooler; she would take her pets for their usual walk in the park and have scrambled eggs for her supper ... She climbed the stairs slowly. Her day had been heavy, the wards were full and because she had to be doubly sure of everything, nursing, as it were, in another language, as well as saying everything twice so that even her monosyllabic remarks could be understood, her work was that much harder. All the same she was happy; her steps quickened as she reached the third landing and got out her key. She could hear Bertie breathing deeply under the door and Pooch uttering the raucous miaouw which was his welcome to her. She opened the door to meet their delighted onslaught.

She fed them first and then, with the promise of a walk, went to take a shower and change into a dress. She was getting a little tired of her scanty wardrobe now; she would buy herself something new in another week, once she had had her first pay packet, in the meantime the blue cotton would have to do. She brushed her hair and left it loose and dug bare feet into sandals. She hadn't bothered overmuch with make-up, it was too warm, but she applied lipstick hurriedly and went in search of Bertie's lead. She was on her knees with her head under the divan when someone knocked on the door and she called 'Kom binnen.' It would be Mevrouw Botte who had promised her some eggs from her daughter's farm.

It wasn't Mevrouw Botte. The Baron strolled in, eyed Becky's lower half sticking out from under the divan and remarked severely: 'You should never tell anyone to come in unless you know who it is, Becky.'

She came out backwards, the lead in her hand, and got to her feet, quite unembarrassed because somehow she never was with him. 'Well, I thought it was Mevrouw Botte with the eggs,' she explained. 'Who else would come here?'

'I would perhaps,' suggested her visitor blandly, and she said quickly:

'Oh, lord—have I done something wrong on the ward? I do try to be careful, but it's such a frightful language, isn't it?'

He agreed gravely and assured her that there was nothing amiss. 'Indeed, everyone is very pleased with your progress.' He looked around him. 'You're comfortable here?'

'Yes, thank you.' Becky looked at him, wondering why he had come.

'Good. I thought that we might go out this evening so that I can catch up on your—er—career.'

She was so surprised that she couldn't think of anything to say. Why should he bother to climb all those stairs just to ask her that when he could have done it much more easily at the hospital?

'Well, that's very kind of you, but I'm not ... I haven't anything to wear.'

The Baron's face remained bland, showing no sign of the rapid changes he was making in his plans for the evening.

'You look just right to me for a picnic.'

Becky's face cleared. 'Oh, a picnic!' She added

soberly: 'But I can't, thank you all the same—Bertie and Pooch, you know, they've been shut up all day and I've promised them a walk in the park.'

'Lola's in the car, they can come too.' He opened the door. 'I've a message from Sutske for Mevrouw Botte—I'll wait for you downstairs.' He paused. 'I quite forgot, Tialda sends her love. If you're free tomorrow she wants to take you out to lunch. Can you manage that?' He smiled faintly at her happy nod. 'And my mother—she sends her love also—she wishes you to have tea with her. Tialda will arrange that, I expect.'

He shut the door quietly behind him and Becky listened to his feet on the stairs. She still couldn't imagine why he had called to see her unless it was a sense of duty, which it most likely was. She put Pooch's harness on and fastened the lead on Bertie's elderly neck, then went out of her little flat, locking the door carefully and with a sense of pride at being able to do so.

The Baron had possessed himself of Mevrouw Botte's telephone and when Willem answered he had given instant and crisp directions: Willem was to cancel the table the Baron had booked for that evening at the exclusive hotel Borg de Breedenburg and ask Sutske to come to the telephone at once. 'I want a picnic basket for two,' he told his housekeeper, 'cold supper and coffee, and tell Willem to put in a bottle of that Moselle—the sweet one.' He had listened patiently to Sutske's scolding voice and when she had finished: 'Dear kind Sutske, you know you don't mean a word of it.'

There was a snort at the other end. 'And you know you never drink that sweet Moselle . . .'

'Just for this once I'm going to, Sutske, do your best—you can have fifteen minutes.'

Sutske snorted again. 'You're no better than when you were a little boy,' she observed sternly and added: 'Willem will be waiting with it, Baron.'

He was in the hall, looking as though he had been waiting for quite some time by the time Becky got there.

It was only a little more than twenty miles to the Baron's house and the road was a good one; the animals shared the back seat and Becky, sitting in front, made polite conversation. It was difficult to think of something to talk about; she didn't think that her companion would be interested in her day-to-day activities, for they hadn't amounted to much so far. She worried away at the weather like a dog with a bone and felt relief when he turned in at the gates and stopped outside the house. 'To collect the picnic,' he told her blandly, and got out to speak to the waiting Willem.

The picnic basket was stowed away in the boot, Willem accorded her a nice smile and retreated to the steps as the Baron started the Rolls. When it was quite out of sight he made his slow way back to the kitchen to remark to Sutske: 'I have never known the master so kindly disposed towards a young lady so lacking in looks and chic, not that she isn't a very nice young lady indeed.' He added deliberately: 'Depend upon it, he is sorry for her.' He heaved a sigh. 'When I think of all the beautiful young ladies he has been interested in . . .'

'It isn't always looks,' observed Sutske darkly, 'though the child could do with more flesh on her bones. I've put in plenty of good food. I wonder where they're going?'

Becky was wondering too. The Baron, carrying on an easy conversation, had taken a side road leading to the coast to the north of his home, presently he turned again on to a narrow dyke road winding between the fields, which led to wooded country a mile or so ahead of them.

'This is pretty,' observed Becky. 'I like trees,' and then, as he turned into an open gateway and on to a sandy lane: 'Oh—isn't this private?'

The Baron's voice was casual. 'Yes, but I know the owner—he has no objection to my coming here.'

A favourite picnicking place for the Baron and Nina, perhaps? Becky stifled a sigh and looked around her. The lane had opened out to a broader road running between meadows, and nicely sheltered by a variety of trees a house stood a little to one side. It was a farmhouse, spick and span with new paint and shining windows and geraniums encircling it like a glowing necklace. As they passed it Becky craned her neck to see it.

'Is it really a farm? It looks so—so well cared for.'

'It is, and it's a farm—pedigree cattle and horses.'

'Your friend's lucky. How lovely to live here—animals and trees—lovely for children.'

'He's not married.'

'He doesn't live here all alone, surely?' She added: 'What a waste!'

'Well, no—he comes here at weekends and during holidays.'

'Oh, poor man—does he work very hard and live away from here, then?'

'He works hard, yes—but he has another house. Probably when he marries he will come out here more often.'

He volunteered no more information but followed the lane away from the meadows back into the trees and surprisingly, on to the dunes with the flat calm sea beyond.

'Oh, it's heaven,' declared Becky. 'Is this where we're going to picnic?'

'I thought it might do. Take Pooch for his walk while I unload the food—the dogs can amuse themselves.'

She wandered off with Pooch ambling along beside her. The air was warm still and smelled of the sea and the trees around her. The sky was a pale, pearly blue and the only sounds were the birds and the happy barking of the dogs. It was perfect, thought Becky, and wondered why she felt vaguely sad. She had no chance to pursue this further though, because the Baron's voice bade her come and eat her supper. She went at once. He had been kind, wasting his evening on her, but she knew better than to keep him waiting.

Sutske had performed miracles in the time the Baron had allowed her; chicken legs wrapped in foil, tiny pork pies, minute sausages, crisp rolls filled with ham and dishes of salad and icecream in a container. There was coffee too in a thermos jug and the

Moselle, packed in its own cooler. Becky sipped it with pleasure and pronounced it delicious, and her companion, swallowing his with no pleasure at all, blandly agreed with her.

Becky sat on the sand, the dogs lolling against her, Pooch on her lap. The sea air had brought colour into her face and the breeze had whipped her hair around her shoulders. The Baron, watching her, was of the opinion that although she hadn't a great deal to be happy about, she was probably the happiest person he had come across for a long time. She looked up and smiled at him. 'All this lovely food,' she said happily, 'although they feed us awfully well at the hospital.'

He filled her plate and passed it to her. 'Ah, yes— tell me about it,' he begged. There was quite a lot to tell, after all, and they had eaten almost everything by the time she had finished answering his questions and, a little hazy with the wine, she leaned back against Bertie's stout body and sighed with content. 'This is the nicest picnic I've ever had,' she told him.

'You make a habit of them?' enquired her companion lazily.

'When I was a little girl, yes—my mother and father and I. Not—not since then.' She kept her voice bright so that he didn't have to feel sorry for her. 'But we picnicked at Molde, didn't we? And that was lovely—I never imagined I'd see Norway; it's funny how life changes suddenly and everything's different ...' She glanced up and saw that he was frowning. She was boring him, rambling on about nothing —she had neither good looks nor conversation. She sat up and began to collect the remains of their meal

with him watching her in silence until she had everything neatly packed away, and when she gave him an
enquiring look he got to his feet, ushered the dogs
back into the car and held the door open for her and
Pooch. He hardly spoke as he drove back, but at her
door he got out too, opened her door and caught
Bertie by his collar. Becky paused on the step, feeling
shy and awkward because she didn't know why he
had become so silent and withdrawn. All the same
she thanked him for her evening, to have her thanks
cut short by his brief: 'I'm coming up.'

The little place was too warm when they reached it
and smaller than ever with the Baron taking up so
much room. Becky switched on the little reading
lamp and said rather defiantly: 'It's rather warm, but
it'll be cosy in the winter. Would you like a cup of
coffee?'

He was leaning against the door, staring at her.
'Thank you, no. You've filled out very nicely, Becky.'

She was so surprised at this that she stared at him,
her mouth open, and then: 'You don't mean that I'm
getting fat?'

The horror in her voice made him laugh. 'No—
only that you're no longer a thin mouse.'

She had nothing to say to that. After a moment she
said: 'It was a lovely evening, thank you very much.
Bertie and Pooch liked it too.'

'And I, Becky? Do you think that I liked it?'

His voice was too silky for her liking but she
answered him seriously: 'Yes, you did, to begin with,
and then I began to bore you, didn't I? The wine, you
know—I'm not used to it and it made me chatty. I'm
sorry it was a wasted evening for you.'

'You're wrong.' His voice was so mild that it didn't sound like his at all. 'I enjoyed every single moment of it, Becky.' He took a step forward and swept her to him with one great arm, kissed her hard and went away, leaving her standing there staring at the closed door. She could hear him running down the stairs, his footsteps getting fainter and fainter. They had died away into silence before she spoke. 'I'm a fool!' she cried, and turned to face Bertie and Pooch, watching her from their box. 'Oh, my dears, do you know what's happened? I'm in love with him—with Tiele—Baron Raukema van den Eck—and I might just as well have fallen in love with the moon!' And she burst into tears.

CHAPTER SEVEN

SHE cried for quite a time, with the animals crowding up close to her, uneasy at the way she was carrying on, but presently she sniffed, blew her red nose and mopped her face. 'You see,' she explained, 'we can't go back to England; I haven't enough money to put you in quarantine and I'd have to get a job, and supposing I met Stepmother or Basil?' She shivered at the thought. 'Besides, I'm happy here, and so are you. I'll just have to keep out of his way, won't I?'

The very idea sent the tears flowing again, so that Pooch, who had wormed his way on to her knees, had to shake his tatty old head free of them.

But presently Becky pulled herself together; crying never did any good. She washed her puffy face and tidied her hair, made a pot of tea and went to bed. And her companions, aware of her misery, broke her strict rule about not getting on to the bed, and crowded on to it with her, making her hotter than ever but offering a silent sympathy which sent her to sleep.

She need not have worried about keeping out of the Baron's way. She didn't see him at all for several days and when she did—on his ward rounds—his austere 'Good morning, Zuster Saunders' would have choked off even the most thick-skinned. She saw him one evening too, driving through the city with Nina beside him, looking utterly beautiful, so that any small silly hopes she had been cherishing died a quick death. She had hurried home, with Bertie plodding along beside her, and spent the evening working away at her Dutch lessons.

She had formed some sort of a plan by now; she would give herself six months in which to learn enough Dutch to make her quite confident of getting another job and move to some other part of Holland. As far away from the Baron as possible, and he need never know where she had gone—probably he wouldn't realise that she had, anyway. In the meantime she made the best of her days. She enjoyed her work now, she had quickly discovered that it was very much the same as it had been in England. Certainly the patients weren't any different even though they spoke a different language. She had made friends too among the nurses and some of the housemen stopped to pass the time of day with her. And the Hoofd Zuster, apparently carved from the same block of granite as the elderly martinet Becky had worked under at Leeds, actually had a heart of gold despite the fact that her tongue was as sharp as a razor and she had the eye of a hawk; she was kind and patient with Becky, never even smiled at her strange mangling of the Dutch language, and after the first week or so, paid her the compliment of speaking to her in Dutch. Not that Becky always understood her; instructions often had to be repeated in English, but at least she was learning, and learning fast.

She had been to tea with the Baroness too, fearful of meeting the Baron there, but he had been at the hospital and despite her hostess's entreaties to stay after tea and meet him, Becky had invented an invitation to the cinema that evening, and left in good time. The Baroness had been kind, and interested in her progress, although a good deal of the visit had been taken up with her own detailed account of her convalescence. She was walking well with a stick now and enlarged at some length on the shopping expeditions she had been able to make. 'Such a pity that Tialda has gone back to den Haag,' she told Becky. 'Pieter came back earlier than she had expected, so of course she went at once.' She sighed. 'So nice to see the child happily married. If only Tiele would marry too—though not,' she added strongly, 'Nina van Doorn.'

'She's a very lovely girl,' offered Becky, putting her paper-thin cup and saucer down because her hand was shaking at the mere thought.

'I know that,' declared the Baroness impatiently. 'It is most unfortunate that she knows it too—her good looks are more important to her than anything or anyone else. Do you know, my dear, that she takes two hours or more to dress? And her clothes—she has far too many.'

That from the Baroness, who had several vast wardrobes full herself, struck Becky as amusing, although she took care not to smile. After all, the little lady sitting opposite her might be spoilt and wilful, but she was kindness itself. Becky said placatingly: 'Well, I don't suppose that your son will mind—he'll be so proud of her.' And then because she couldn't bear to go on talking about him any more, she made her excuses, hurrying through the streets, anxious not to meet the Baron.

But she had to meet him sooner or later. Only a few days later she was on duty when he came into the ward, and because the other nurses were at their coffee, Becky was told to join the procession behind him to fulfil the humble duty of pulling curtains round the patient to be examined, support her while the examination took place, and arrange the bed-clothes just so afterwards. It was unfortunate that the patients to be seen that day were, for the most part, well built ladies who needed heaving up against their pillows and sustained there while the Baron went carefully over their chests. It was difficult to keep out of his way while he was doing so and even harder to keep her head from bumping his and quite impossible upon occasion to prevent their hands touching. Becky's small nose twitched at the expensive cologne the Baron favoured and did her best to ignore him, something he had no difficulty in doing. She might not have been there; even when he looked at her, his blue eyes went right through her to some distant point of concentration while he probed and poked gently. And indeed, she had proof of this later that day, when she met him on the stairs. He had stopped to bid her a courteous good day and added: 'How are you getting on, Becky? I haven't seen you lately.'

She had steadied her breath and replied that she was getting on very well, thank you, before ducking her head awkwardly at him and galloping past him to lose herself in the blessed hordes of people milling round in Outpatients where she had been sent to help out for the afternoon.

The fine weather broke a few days later, the blue sky shut out by great storm clouds hovering menacingly, occasionally drenching everyone beneath them with warm rain. Becky, plodding home wet and tired, decided that she would rather suffer the heat of her little flat than be cool and have no view from its windows but wet roofs. It was only a little past six o'clock, but it was ominously dark and still. There would be a storm soon, she decided, and hurried even faster. She was standing in the doorway shaking herself like a wet dog, when the basement door opened and Mevrouw Botte joined her. Becky smiled and greeted her and wondered why she looked so very agitated; she was casting about for the right words to ask when her landlady spoke. 'Bertie——' she began, and went on slowly so that Becky would understand. 'He has gone, one hour, two hours ago. It is my fault, Miss Saunders, I went to your flat to close the door because of the rain, you understand, and he ran from the room and before I could get downstairs he had disappeared.' She added: 'The cat is safe.'

Becky stood saying nothing, thinking of all the awful things which could have happened to old Bertie, wandering about in a strange town and not even understanding if someone spoke to him. She had taken off her raincoat to shake it, but now she put it back on again. She said in her slow awkward Dutch: 'I'll go and look for him, he can't be very far away—perhaps he's in the park.'

She went back up the street, looking down the narrow *steegs* leading from it as she went and crossing to the canal side to peer down its banks. And in the park, she combed every bush and corner, whistling all the time and listening for Bertie's gruff old voice. But there was no sign of him and she forced herself to stand a minute and consider where he might be. Run over, lying in some gutter; wounded and unable to move, taken by someone and sold to a laboratory ... her mind boggled at horrors and returned to normal good sense again. He was a sensible dog, even though old, so possibly he was sheltering from the rain and if she didn't find him soon she would go to the police station. She went back to the house to find Mevrouw Botte hovering unhappily on her doorstep and shaking her head mournfully, and stopping only to ask her to keep an eye open for him, Becky hurried off again. Bertie liked water, he had once or twice ventured down the canal's banks to gaze at its murky waters at close quarters. She walked the length of the street, whistling and calling and searching every inch of the canal before running down a side street leading to a much wider thoroughfare bisected by a much wider canal, frequently crossed by bridges. She was running over the first of these when she ran full tilt into the Baron.

'What the devil are you doing?' he demanded, 'tearing along like a street urchin!'

Becky hardly stopped. 'Bertie's lost.' She got another yard or two before he took her by the arm and swung her round.

'No, don't pull away like that—when did he go?'

'About two hours ago—Mevrouw Botte isn't sure. He ran through the door when she went to close the windows.' She gulped. 'I've searched the park and the street.' She tugged at her arm. 'Let me go, do!' She

ended on a small shriek because the storm broke then
with a vivid flash of lightning and a great rumble of
thunder which drowned every other sound.

The Baron turned up the collar of his Burberry.
'You go down that side, I'll search this—we'll find
him, Becky. You're not afraid of the storm?'

She was terrified, but her terror was quite wiped
out by anxiety for Bertie. She shook her head and
started off down the deserted street, peering through
the pelting rain, searching the canal as well as every
doorway and alley. She could see the Baron on the
other side, doing exactly the same thing, and it made
her feel a little better. He had disappeared down a
steeg when she reached the next bridge, larger than
the rest, its supports crowded with a mass of broken
wood, old boxes and tangles of wire, caught up in a
hopeless mess until someone should come and clear
them away. It was so gloomy now that she couldn't
see very clearly right under the bridge, but her heart
gave a leap when she heard a faint whine. She clam-
bered down to the canal's edge and saw Bertie,
wedged in with all the rubbish. She whistled encour-
agingly and called him, but he only whined again,
and another flash of lightning which made her cringe
with fright showed her that he was unable to get free.

The water looked filthy; she peeled off her soaking
raincoat and slid off the bank and began to swim towards the bridge. She was almost there when she
remembered that it would have been a good idea to
have warned the Baron; he would come out of his
steeg and see that she wasn't on the opposite bank.
She could shout, of course, but the chance of getting
a mouthful of the vile water she was swimming

through was too great. She reached the first of the old spars which comprised the perimeter of the flotsam upon which Bertie was trapped, and trod water.

He was delighted to see her although he didn't bark. From what she could see of him, he was soaking wet and tired out. She took a deep breath and shouted: 'I'm here!' and nearly let go of her spar when the Baron said quietly from behind her, 'A good thing I saw you sliding into the water. I take it Bertie's trapped in some way.'

They worked their way closer to Bertie, who showed his teeth for a moment and then kept still while the Baron gently prised him loose from the wire, the wood and a couple of nasty rusty nails embedded in his hind leg.

'Right,' he said at length, 'it's impossible to see if he's injured in any other way. I'll swim him back—you go and get your raincoat and come over the bridge.'

Becky hadn't spoken; she had been so happy to have found Bertie again that she hadn't really noticed the slimy water or the storm raging around her. But now the thought of going even those few yards and then chancing more lightning and thunder appalled her. Her teeth chattered with her fright and the Baron said briskly: 'Go on, you'll catch your death of cold if you don't look sharp.'

So she swam back and crawled up the bank and put on her raincoat which seemed a bit silly since she was wet to the bone, and then ran back over the bridge, gasping and wincing at the storm and almost knocked over by the rain.

The Baron was waiting for her with Bertie over

one shoulder. At Becky's scared look he said hearteningly: 'He's not too bad, but he's limping and it will be quicker to carry him. Thank God it isn't far.'

He tucked his free hand under her arm and started off, not speaking at all excepting when they got to Mevrouw Botte's door when he let her go to push her gently inside before him. 'Lord, how we smell!' he exclaimed, and Becky was surprised to see that he was laughing. She burst out laughing too and Mevrouw Botte, waiting for them anxiously in the open doorway, looked at them both with astonishment. She would have asked a lot of questions, but the Baron cut her short with a smile and began mounting the stairs, Becky in front and Bertie, moaning gently, still draped on his shoulders. On the tiny landing he took the key from her hand and opened the door, pushed her before him and then laid the dog carefully on the hearthrug.

'Warm water and soap,' he demanded unhurriedly, 'and I'll wash some of this stuff off me before I begin on Bertie. While I'm seeing to him supposing you have a shower and get into something dry?'

He took off his jacket and went to the sink and Becky exclaimed: 'Your raincoat ...'

'I'll telephone Willem presently; he can fetch it.' He grinned suddenly. 'You look simply frightful, my dear, but you're a very brave girl.'

It wasn't the kind of compliment a girl would appreciate, but it was better than nothing, she supposed. 'Now get those wet things off,' he ordered.

'Yes—but Bertie ...?'

'He'll do, I fancy. I'm going to clean him up and then send for the vet.'

She took slacks and a sweater from the cupboard and presently, her hair still damp round her shoulders, joined him on the floor by Bertie.

The Baron had done a good job on the old dog. He was clean and almost dry and his wounded leg was lying on what Becky recognised as one of Mevrouw Botte's pillowcases. She asked urgently: 'Shall I telephone now? And what about you?'

His mouth twitched faintly. 'No. I'll telephone—the vet and Willem, he can bring me some clothes. I'll ask Mevrouw Botte if I can use her shower. I'll be back before the vet goes.'

Left alone Becky hugged Bertie gently, fed an impatient Pooch and tidied up the mess the Baron had made. She had only just finished this when the vet arrived—a cheerful young man who introduced himself as de Viske and began work on Bertie without more ado. 'Tiele around?' he wanted to know.

'He's downstairs, changing his clothes—he came into the canal too, you see.'

Mijnheer de Viske didn't see at all; it wasn't like Tiele to go grovelling around in canals, but he supposed there had been some good reason for it. He asked: 'Did the dog fall in the water?'

'Well, we don't know—he was lost and then we found him caught up in a lot of flotsam under a bridge.'

He would get the story out of Tiele later. In the meantime he examined Bertie, cleaned his injured leg, put a couple of stitches in and gave him an antibiotic. 'He'll do,' he pronounced finally. 'Keep him quiet for a day or two. I'll come round and take another look in a day or two—Tiele's got my telephone number if you should want me before then,'

Becky thanked him, wondering if she should tell him that she wasn't on those sort of terms with the Baron; she was wondering, too, how best to say so when that gentleman, in slacks and a sweater, came in, to engage Mijnheer de Viske in a brief conversation before he left. Becky, who had expected the Baron to go at the same time, was nonplussed when he sat himself down in a shabby, comfortable easy chair by the empty stove, lifted Pooch on to his knee and asked in the mildest of voices if there was any coffee.

And when she said yes, she would make it straight away: 'And I hope you can make it in the Dutch way—it's mostly undrinkable in England.'

She hurried to assure him that Mevrouw Botte had taught her exactly how to make it and went into her little kitchen, to pop out a minute later to answer the knock on the door. It was Willem bearing a tray loaded with bottle and glasses. He wished her good evening in a benign voice, expressed the hope that she was none the worse for her adventure and still speaking English informed his master that he was about to return to Huize Raukema; that he had found the raincoat, fetched the Rolls from the hospital where it had been parked, and added in an expressionless voice: 'And Juffrouw van Doorn, Baron, is there any message for her?'

The Baron gazed at his elderly friend and servant, looking remarkably put out. He said something which sounded like the worst kind of swear words in a forceful voice, and Becky was sorry that she couldn't understand them. It was obvious that Willem did,

though, from the shocked look on his face. But the
Baron recovered quickly. He said blandly: 'Ah, yes
—I had forgotten, think up something for me, will
you, Willem? If you could tell her that I have been
unavoidably detained— and she had better go without me, and make my excuses.'

'Very good, *mijnheer*.' Willem's face was as bland
as his master's as he poured the brandy, asked if there
was anything else he could do and bade them both
good evening.

'He's very nice,' pronounced Becky. 'Have you had
him a very long time?'

The Baron handed her a glass. 'Legend has it that
I sat on his knee as a baby.'

Becky tried to imagine her companion as a baby
and failed completely. 'I'm sorry your evening has
been spoilt; I hope Juffrouw van Doorn won't be too
upset.'

'She will be livid,' he observed with calm. 'Drink
your brandy, it will prevent you catching cold.' He
leant over Bertie for a moment and listened to the
dog's snores. 'He'll be all right now.'

Becky sipped her brandy, wrinkling her nose. 'This
tastes very peculiar.'

Not a muscle of the Baron's face moved. He would
hardly have described his best Napoleon brandy as
peculiar. He said merely: 'I think that it is a taste
that one acquires.' He got up from his chair, putting
Pooch gently on the floor, and went to stand by the
door. 'You are still happy at the hospital? It has
seemed to me that the work may be too heavy for
you ...'

She felt herself grow pale; she hadn't been satis-

factory after all, and she had been trying so hard.
'No, I don't mean that you aren't able to do the work
—you seem to be getting on very nicely, I merely
meant that the patients you heave up and down their
beds seem to be at least three times your size. I
thought that old Mevrouw Kats would have had you
on the floor ...'

Becky went red where she had been white before.
She hadn't thought he had seen her and he had. 'I'm
very strong.' She took another sip of the brandy, and
then another. She didn't like the taste, but it was de-
liciously warming. A pleasant cosy haze slowly en-
veloped her; she had tried very hard during the last
few days to forget the Baron, but it had been of no
use, of course, and the effort had given her a per-
petual headache and kept her awake at night, but
now she suddenly felt quite cheerful.

'I haven't thanked you yet,' she said chattily. 'I—
we're awfully grateful—it would have been quite a
job prising Bertie loose on my own.' She took another
sip. 'I didn't know you walked ... I mean, you always
seem to be going or coming in your car.' She added,
to make it quite clear: 'Sometimes I see you going
back from the hospital, you often have Juffrouw van
Doorn with you.'

He stared at her, his eyes very blue. 'Yes?'

The brandy had gone to Becky's head. 'You really
shouldn't marry her, you know—she's not the wife
for you.'

The Baron shifted his position slightly and took a
drink. 'Should I not?' he queried softly. 'Pray give
me your advice, my dear girl.'

His voice should have warned her, but she was

now in a state of euphoria beyond heeding that. Her eyes had grown very dark and round and she spoke with careful deliberation. 'Someone kind and loving who would take no notice of your bad temper; who'd look after you and make sure that you had enough sleep, and ...'

'My God!' exploded the Baron. 'And this paragon? Will she be as beautiful as she is good? Clever and amusing and exciting too, I suppose.' He paused and went on bitingly, his eyes like blue ice: 'Or should she be a skinny creature with no conversation —such as yourself, Rebecca?'

It seemed as though all the blood in her body was rushing to her face. She felt her cheeks burn, but worse than that was the humiliation. Her ever-returning hopes that he might like her were buried under it. He didn't like her, but did he have to be so cruel, even though she had been a fool to talk to him like that? It was entirely her own fault, she shouldn't have drunk that brandy. She made herself meet his eyes without flinching.

'Of course she would be beautiful and amusing because you—you never look at anyone less than that, do you? But she could be kind too.' She drew a breath and put the empty glass down carefully on the crochet mat Mevrouw Botte considered correct to display on the table. She said miserably, wishing she could still her unruly tongue: 'I'm sorry I said that, it was only because I like you so much that I did it. I'd like you to be happy ...' Her voice trailed away under his mocking look.

'You're drunk, my dear. A glass of brandy and probably no supper. Go to bed and sleep it off. I should keep to tea, if I were you.' He put his glass down beside hers, wished her goodnight and ran down the stairs, in such a hurry he didn't shut the door behind him. Becky shut it slowly and then went and sat by the dozing Bertie. Presently Pooch came to sit with her and she stayed there a long while, so unhappy that she was quite beyond tears.

She made tea later, saw to Bertie's and Pooch's needs and got ready for bed. She was on the point of putting out the light when Mevrouw Botte knocked on the door and when Becky opened it, handed her a note.

'Willem,' she said, and pointed downstairs. It was a brief missive, telling her, in the Baron's careless unintelligible scrawl, that he had arranged with the hospital that she should take her days off on the next two days so that Bertie might have the necessary attention. It had no beginning and no end, just his initials.

She told herself that she must be grateful for his thoughtfulness and went to bed, where she spent an almost sleepless night wondering how she would feel when she saw him again. Absolutely ghastly, she supposed.

The two days went slowly. She tended Bertie, who was making a remarkable recovery, easing him up and down the stairs twice a day with Pooch under her arm, doing a little household shopping and trying out her Dutch, and working at her lessons. The weather had cleared after the storm, but it was cooler now, so that the little room under the roof was quite bearable, besides, she could take a chair on to the balcony when she felt inclined. But it was dull too and she couldn't be bothered to cook, so that on the third day, when she went back to work, she had got thinner and there were dark shadows under her eyes because she hadn't been sleeping. She tried not to think about meeting the Baron; she would have to sooner or later, she knew that, but it would be easier if it were during a ward round when he had no need to address her. Perhaps Fate would be kind, she thought hopefully, as she darted down the corridor on her way to the changing room.

Fate was nothing of the sort. Coming towards her was the Baron. And why here? she thought wildly; it doesn't lead anywhere but the cloakrooms and Nurses' Home. She took a few deep breaths so that by the time he had reached her she was able to say good morning in a quiet voice. She had had every intention of not stopping, indeed, she had passed him when he caught her by the shoulder and brought her to a halt.

'How is Bertie?' he wanted to know.

'Very much better, thank you. Mr de Viske is coming this afternoon to see him.' She wriggled a little under his hand. 'I'm on duty ...'

'Not so fast. My mother has Tialda staying with her, and they would like you to go to tea. Tomorrow?'

'I'm sorry, it's my two to eight.'

'In that case, make it lunch. Ulco shall fetch you at half past eleven—my mother will be lunching at noon. You will be taken back in good time so that you can look in on Bertie before you go on duty.'

'I don't think ...' began Becky weakly.

'She will be delighted to see you again,' said the

Baron smoothly, 'and Tialda is only here until to-morrow evening.' He nodded briefly and was gone before she could say another word.

She saw him later on the round, of course; he in-cluded her in his general good morning to the small group of people waiting to accompany him. It was a pity that several of the patients were even heavier than Mevrouw Kats and one of them stone deaf into the bargain. Becky was forced to raise her voice so that she might give instructions to the old dear, tying her tongue in knots over the grammar while the Baron stood at the foot of the bed, looking impassive and, she had no doubt, laughing his head off.

She was ready in good time the next morning, al-though she wasn't absolutely sure that the Baron had meant a word of his invitation. But Ulco arrived exactly at half past eleven, expressed his pleasure at seeing her again and ushered her into the Cadillac, as thought she were royalty. Indeed, on the short jour-ney to the Baroness's house, he told her that she had been very much missed and that everyone would be glad to see her again.

And the Baroness's greeting bore this out. She de-clared that she didn't see nearly enough of Becky and that something must be done about it, and when Tialda joined them presently she hugged Becky with real pleasure, declaring that she would have to pay her a visit in den Haag before the summer was out. So it was a cheerful little party which sat down to a delicious lunch presently, and Becky, after her un-inspired diet of fruit and bread and cheese and too many cups of tea, ate with appetite. Just at first she had been on tenterhooks, afraid that the Baron would join them, and it was a relief when Tialda mentioned that she had met Nina in town and been told that Tiele was taking her to lunch. 'At least,' went on Tialda, 'she invited herself—she told me so. I wish Tiele would exert himself ... she practically lives with him, and only because he's too lazy to do anything about it. He won't marry her, of course—he's not quite such a fool, but I just wish he'd fall in love with someone else.' She smiled at Becky. 'Have you made any friends yet, Becky?'

'Well, I'm getting to know some of the nurses—it'll be better when I can speak Dutch properly.'

'Oh, good—I must come and see your flat one day, but now Pieter's back I don't have much time.'

Becky said she didn't suppose that she had and asked the Baroness how she was getting on—an endless topic which lasted until it was time for her to leave. 'If you don't mind?' she asked her hostess. 'You see, I must just pop in and make sure Bertie is all right.'

The Baroness kissed her. 'And next time you must come for the day and bring Bertie and Pooch. Tialda, you must try and come too.'

Ulco was waiting in the hall. So was the Baron, and when she stopped short: 'Well, don't look so surprised, Becky—I happened to be passing and it seemed good sense to pick you up.' He ushered her through the door Ulco had opened for them and opened the door of the Rolls. Nina was in the front seat. She turned her head and nodded without speaking as Becky got in and when Tiele was beside her again, spoke to him in Dutch, making Becky well aware that she was being given a lift and nothing more. Although the Baron didn't seem to consider that to be the case, because he asked her how she thought his mother was getting on, wanted to know if Bertie had quite recovered and even made one or two observations about the hospital, so that Nina had no chance to join in the conversation. At Mevrouw Botte's door he stopped, remarking: 'I'll wait for you, Becky—is ten minutes enough?'

She was already out of the car as he came round to her door. 'Thank you, but I'll walk.' She was breathing rather fast and her colour was high; Nina hadn't even bothered to turn her head when she had wished her goodbye.

'Why?' He smiled faintly. 'You'll be late on duty.'

'I prefer to be that than—than ... I suppose you think it's funny to watch her snubbing me—I expect you think I deserve it, too. Probably I do. Thank you for the lift.'

She couldn't walk away because he had taken her by the arm. Now he turned and said something to Nina which made that young lady sizzle with temper. 'I've told Nina that she can wait if she likes to. Let's go up.'

But before he did he took the ignition key out of the car and put it into a pocket, blandly ignoring both girls' astonished faces.

Inside the flat he sat down, watching Becky putting food out and opening the door on to the balcony. 'And let me assure you, Becky, that I don't find Nina's behaviour towards you in the least funny. I'm not sure what I find it.' He bent to lift an impatient Pooch on to his knee. 'That's not quite true, but there is no time to discuss it now. Are you ready?'

Nina had gone by the time they reached the car. 'Get in front,' begged the Baron. 'We can talk shop until we get to the hospital.'

Which they did in a comfortable casual fashion, brought to an end when they were crossing the vast entrance hall together.

'I should prefer it if you were to call me Tiele,' said the Baron à propos nothing.

Becky would have stopped if he had given her the chance, but as he didn't she contented herself with a long look at him. 'Quite impossible—you're a Baron and a doctor, and I worked for you ...'

'I wish you wouldn't keep throwing Baron at me in that inflexible fashion; I was Tiele first, you know. Besides, you told me that you liked me ...'

She marched on, not looking at him, her cheeks glowing. 'I like you, too, Becky.' His voice was beguiling.

She said stonily: 'Yes, I know. I heard you telling your mother that in Trondheim—you liked me, but I wasn't your cup of tea.'

'And I was quite right—but I do believe that you're my glass of champagne, Becky.'

They had come to a halt now, for she had to turn down a corridor leading to the back of the hospital and he was going, presumably, to the consultants' room. In any case, a houseman was hovering, only kept at bay by the Baron's dismissing wave of the hand.

'I don't understand you at all,' declared Becky severely.

'I'm not sure that I understand myself.' He added

sharply: 'You've got thin again, are you eating enough?'

'Yes, thank you. I-I expect it's the warm weather.'

He nodded, thinking about something else. Then: 'You have enough money?'

Becky was vexed to feel her cheeks grow hot again. 'Yes, thank you.'

'And yet you seem to have very few clothes. I thought girls spent a lot of money on clothes.'

Her eye caught the clock; she had about three minutes in which to change and present herself on the ward. 'Oh, we do, but I-I'm saving up for something.' She gave a funny indecisive little nod, said goodbye and flew along the corridor. If he had asked what she was saving up for she would have had to tell a fib— she was normally an honest girl, but to look him in the eye and tell him that she was saving every cent so that she could get away from him just wasn't on.

CHAPTER EIGHT

BECKY saw a good deal of the Baron during the next week; they seemed to be forever meeting on stairs and along corridors and he came to the ward frequently, often on his own, and twice he left when she did, offering her a lift home which she accepted, because although her head reminded her of her resolve not to see him unless she was forced to, her heart urged her to turn a deaf ear to such advice. And on the second occasion he had suggested, vaguely, she had to admit, that he would take her to dine at a famous castle hotel—Borg de Breedenburg, which was at Warffum, a village about fifteen miles north of Groningen. On the strength of his suggestion she had gone out the very next day and bought a dress, a pretty flowered cotton voile which cost a good deal more than she could afford, telling herself that she was a fool to have taken him seriously.

An assumption which proved to be only too true. She didn't see him at all for two days and on the third day, although he did a ward round, he didn't appear to see her. She had hardly expected him to stop and speak to her on the ward, but he could surely have managed a smile. She went down to her dinner in a temper, made worse by her unhappiness. He had forgotten, or worse, merely made a casual remark which hadn't meant a thing. She pranced down the staircase, frowning fiercely, and walked right into Wim Tolde, one of the junior housemen who had from time to time spoken to her. He stopped now and caught her by the arm.

'Hey, what is wrong with you, Zuster Becky? So cross, and such a frown.' He smiled at her kindly. 'You are having a bad day?' And when she nodded: 'Then something must be done—I have tickets for the concert in the Town Hall this evening, my girl-friend cannot come and I would be glad if you will accompany me instead; I do not like to be alone.'

Becky hesitated; she accepted the fact that he was asking her because he wanted someone to go with, not because it was her as a person, but he was a nice boy, still scared stiff because he had only just qualified, and it would be an excuse to wear the new dress, too. She said that yes, she would like to go very much, thank you.

Wim seemed pleased. 'I must go now.' He turned on his heel and called over his shoulder: 'I will be at the front entrance at seven o'clock. Do not be late—I don't want to miss a single moment . . .'

Becky wondered why he suddenly looked so uncomfortable, staring over her shoulder and then hurrying away and she turned round to see. The Baron was quite close, a few yards from her; he must have heard every word. He said quietly: 'You are going out this evening?'

Becky nodded. 'Yes. To a concert.' And then because he looked so bad-tempered about it, added defiantly: 'I like going out, too.'

'Meaning?'

'Just exactly that, sir.'

He frowned down at her. 'You go out often? I somehow imagined ...' He looked quite fierce. 'I hope you choose your friends carefully, Becky.'

She said steadily: 'You have been very kind to me, I can't forget that, but you don't have to feel responsible for me any more, you know—I'm making my own life now.'

She couldn't tell from his face what he was thinking; it was impassive as it so often was. He said merely: 'Of course, Becky,' and went past her, up the stairs.

There was no pleasure in putting on the new dress. She had bought it because she was going out with Tiele, and now she wasn't and there was really no reason to dress up for Wim; he already had a girlfriend and besides, she hadn't the least interest in him. All the same she met him with a cheerful smile exactly on time and walked with him to the Town Hall, listening to his rather pompous remarks about his work. He was going to carve a career for himself, he told her, so that he and his Elsa could get married; he had done well in his exams and very soon his superiors would realise how clever he was—another year on the medical side and then a junior partnership if he could get the money together. 'Of course, Doctor Raukema van den Eck could help me. He has great influence—he knows everybody of importance ...' Wim puffed out his chest. 'One day I shall be as important as he is, too, although of course I am not of the *Adel*.'

'Surely that doesn't have anything to do with being a good doctor?'

'No, of course not, but he has much money and is greatly respected.' He added honestly: 'He is also a very good doctor.'

'I had noticed.'

The Gemeente Huis was packed. It wasn't until they were seated in the middle of the seats on the ground floor that Becky saw that there was a gallery encircling them above; presumably the élite were to sit there, as there were flowers arranged along the balcony's edge and the seats looked more comfortable than the hard wooden one she was seated on. She accepted the programme Wim handed to her and read it slowly, realising with horror that it was chamber music, something she had never enjoyed, moreover the works of Bach, Handel and somebody called Antonio de Cabezon, of whom she had never even heard, predominated throughout the lengthy programme. She was a little cheered to see that there was a list of vocalists at the end. A little singing would help the evening along and at least she could study the lady singers' dresses.

Sitting silently beside Wim, who was taking no notice of her at all, she listened to an unaccompanied work by Bach for violin and cello and presently cautiously looked around her. Everyone there was gazing raptly at the group of players on the platform—that was, everyone but the Baron. She saw him at once, sitting behind a bank of nicely arranged carnations, next to a stout lady who had her eyes shut. He was staring down at her and even in the semi-dark he looked bad-tempered. Becky returned her gaze to the

players, composing her unremarkable features into
what she hoped was a look of intense interest, and
kept it like that until the music ended, when she
clapped just as heartily as those around her, though
for a different reason.

'A splendid rendering,' pronounced Wim. 'Bach
expressed his deeper thoughts in such works, do you
not think so?'

Becky looked wise and said, oh, yes, of course and
kept her interested gaze on him while he went over
the performance, note by note. When the lights were
lowered and the musicians were well and truly into
the next item she turned her head very slowly and
peered upwards. The Baron was staring down at her
again and she allowed her eyes to turn casually from
one side to the other as though she hadn't seen him,
before riveting them on the platform once again. It
was a long composition and except for a nervous
cough from time to time, she could have heard a pin
drop. The audience was attentive, nobody around
her moved a muscle. Presently she looked down on
to her lap and allowed her thoughts to wander. Now
if it had been Sibelius or Shostakovich or Brahms she
would have loved every moment of it. She sighed
soundlessly; she had no culture; she knew very little
about anything and in a country where everyone
seemed to speak English as easily as their own
tongue, she was the complete ignoramus. The lights
went up and she concentrated on trying to understand
what Wim was saying about the origin of chamber
music : 'And it is singing next,' he told her. 'You will
enjoy that.'

The soloists filed on to the platform, a stout man

in white tie and tails and two ladies in flowered tents. Becky had no doubt at all that they had excellent voices, but as they sang in German and it was a madrigal, she found her interest wandering. She turned a little in her chair so that she could peep upwards without it noticing. The Baron was sitting back with his eyes closed and now she saw Nina, until that moment hidden behind a massive arrangement of summer flowers next to him. She was looking bored and for once Becky felt strongly sympathetic towards her, although the feeling didn't last long. Even at that distance she looked shatteringly lovely.

The singing ended, giving way to an interval during which almost everyone went into the foyer where there was a bar, but Wim stayed where he was, pointing out that there was such a crowd that their chance of getting anything to drink was small; they might just as well sit quietly where they were and discuss the performance. As far as Becky could see, everyone in the gallery had disappeared. Perhaps they were privileged and had a bar of their own ... She lent an attentive ear to Wim's knowledgeable remarks and wondered if he would take her to supper afterwards —or at least a cup of coffee; she had had only a snatched tea and she was famished.

She managed not to look up once during the second half of the concert and even when the lights went on at its end she kept her eyes fixed on the people around her. Wim looked at his watch. 'It's after ten o'clock,' he told her. 'We'd better get a tram; I'm on early duty in the morning.'

Becky agreed, outwardly cheerful while her insides rumbled, and followed him through the press of people to the street outside. When a hand fell on her shoulder she jumped, trod on someone's foot, apologised and turned round.

'A delightful concert, was it not?' queried the Baron courteously. 'Such splendid voices, and I particularly enjoyed the oboe.' Wim had stopped, looking awkward, and the Baron went on smoothly: 'Ah, young Tolde, is it not? You are together? I'll give you a lift back.'

He bore them inexorably forward, to be joined by Nina who had been talking to a group of people on the pavement. She looked annoyed when she saw them and still more annoyed when the Baron said briskly: 'Nina, I'm going to drop these two off.' They had reached the Rolls and he was opening doors and stuffing them inside so that no one had a chance to say much. 'I'll go to your place first. I'm afraid we'll have to call off supper, Nina, something's come up and I must get back to the hospital.' He turned round and addressed Wim. 'You first, Tolde. We can go past the hospital on the way.' He seemed to have forgotten Becky.

Nina had a good deal to say, but Becky's Dutch wasn't up to understanding it, but she was annoyed, that was certain. She sat rigid presently while the Baron drove through Leeuwarden, deposited Wim at the hospital gates and then drove on again to a quiet street where he pulled up before a block of modern flats and got out with Nina. He wasn't gone long, and when he got back he drove off again without speaking to Becky, still sitting in the back. She wondered if she should give a polite cough or say something light like: 'I'm still here,' or 'I can walk home from here,' when he asked: 'Are you hungry, Becky?'

She said yes before she could stop herself and he said: 'Good, so am I—let's eat.'

'But you've got to go to the hospital—you said something had come up ...'

'So it has, but not at the hospital. It's too late to go to Waffum—we'll go to the Pannekoekhuysje and eat pancakes.'

Which they did—enormous ones, a foot across, liberally sprinkled with crisp fat bacon, and lavishly damped down with black treacle. Becky, who hadn't believed the Baron when he had described what he had ordered for them both, took a first mouthful in some doubt and then quickly decided that she had never tasted anything so suitable for an empty stomach. They washed it down with lager because, as it was explained to her, that was the correct drink to have with a *spek Pannekoek*. They didn't bother to talk much to begin with. Only when they were half way through did Becky put down her knife and fork and observe: 'This is absolutely delicious!'

'Ah, but you should eat it on a raw winter's day when the frost's thick on the ground and your feet are frozen—there's nothing like it then.'

Becky tried to imagine Nina sitting in her place, making inroads into the wholesome fattening food on her plate, and found it impossible. The Baron's voice interrupted her thoughts. 'You enjoyed the concert this evening?'

She cast around for an answer that wasn't exactly a fib. 'Well—I don't know much about Bach or—or madrigals ...'

'And yet you appeared to be deeply absorbed—perhaps it was the flowered tents which interested you so much.'

Her eyes widened with laughter. 'Oh, that's what I called them too—they were, weren't they?'

'Why did you go?' The Baron lifted a finger and ordered coffee.

'Well, I thought it would be nice to go out.' She sounded wistful without knowing it. 'I didn't know what kind of concert it was, though. If it had been Brahms or Sibelius I'd have loved it.'

'Ah—a romantic. I must say I prefer them myself—the madrigal has never been my favourite form of music.'

'Then why did you go?'

When he answered 'Because you did,' she goggled at him in amazement.

'But Nina was there, I saw her ...'

'The poor girl! She had been expecting to visit one of her dear friends' birthday party.'

Becky giggled despite herself. 'Do you mean to say you took her to the concert without her knowing she was going?'

'Something like that.' He smiled at her and her heart melted against her ribs. 'Why?' she asked in a whisper.

He stared at her across the table, his eyes very blue and bright. 'You know, Becky, I do believe that we are at last establishing a good relationship—isn't that the modern jargon? Do you realise that we have been sitting here for upwards of an hour without a cross word to show for it? I must be a reformed character.'

He didn't give her a chance to answer him but went on smoothly:

'Has de Viske been to see Bertie?'

It seemed best to ignore the first part of his remark. 'Yes—he's pleased with him, he told me that Bertie was a fine healthy dog for his age—he gave me some pills for him. He looked at Pooch too, he said he might as well while he was there.' She frowned faintly, thinking of the bill which hadn't come yet; she shouldn't have bought the new dress—a thought instantly cancelled out by the Baron's quiet:

'I like that thing you're wearing—you should wear pretty things more often, Becky.'

She finished her coffee and didn't say anything. Probably he had no idea what it cost to live, especially when you had two animals and were trying to save. 'If you don't mind, I think I ought to go home. I'm on at ten o'clock and I must take Bertie for his walk first and I've the shopping to do. Thank you for my supper.'

In the car he asked her: 'Do you like young Tolde?'

'Like him? He's all right, and he was kind when I first started work—stopped to talk to me and showed me where the dining room was when I got lost. His girl-friend couldn't come this evening and he just wanted company.'

The Baron said: 'Ah, just so.' He sounded so satisfied that she glanced at his profile in surprise, but it gave nothing away.

When they reached Mevrouw Botte's house he got out too. 'I'll take Bertie to stretch his legs while you make the coffee,' he told her, and followed her up the stairs.

Becky had had no intention of asking him in for coffee, but she found herself getting the pot from the kitchen shelf and going through the careful ritual. It was ready when he got back with Bertie, who sat down at once and looked starved until she offered a biscuit, which meant that Pooch had to have something too. The Baron poured milk into a saucer and then accepted his coffee. 'A very pleasant evening,' he pronounced, 'and full of surprises.'

'Surprises? I don't think I was surprised.'

'They were all surprises for me,' he told her, which explained nothing, and put his coffee cup down. 'You're growing into quite a pretty girl, Becky.'

She shook her head sadly. 'No, I'm not, thank you all the same.' She added quite fiercely: 'I wish I were beautiful, so that everyone stared at me ...'

She looked away, ashamed of her outburst so that she didn't see his smile.

'There are so many kinds of beauty—have you ever looked in a small hidden pool in a wood, Becky? It's full of beauty, but it's not in the least spectacular, only restful and quiet and never-endingly fascinating.' He got up and wandered to the door. 'Someone said—and I've forgotten who—"Beauty is nothing other than the promise of happiness." That's very true, you know.'

He put out an arm and pulled her close and kissed her gently. 'Good night, my pretty little mouse.'

A remark which gave Becky a sleepless night.

It was silly to get up ten minutes earlier so that she could take pains with her face and hair, especially as the Baron wasn't to be seen all day—nor the day after, for that matter. On the third day, while she was having coffee with some of her new friends, she ventured to ask casually if Doctor Raukema van den Eck had beds in other hospitals.

'But of course,' she was told. 'He has beds in Groningen, and he goes often to Utrecht and Leiden, for he lectures also. And as well as that he goes often to England; he is a busy man. He is in England now, I think.'

'And does the so lovely Nina van Doorn go with him?' asked a voice, and Becky let out a relieved breath which she hadn't known she had been holding when someone else said: 'No, because I saw her yesterday with a man—he was old, at least fifty, and fat. They were being driven in a Mercedes limousine.'

The speaker turned to Becky. 'You have met this Nina? She is very beautiful, is she not? She is also greedy for money, therefore she is always to be seen with Doctor Raukema, who has a great deal of it. But perhaps this fat man has more. I hope so.' There was general laughter in which Becky joined, praying quietly that the fat man would be a multi-millionaire. The Baron might be rich, but surely not as rich as all that.

He was back the next morning, coming on to the ward with his usual followers. Becky had seen him through the linen room door while she sorted sheets for the beds which had to be made up for the new admissions, so she stayed where she was until she judged that he would be well started—she could sneak up and along the other side and into the side ward.

Which she did, and since he had his back to her, she felt safe in assuming that he hadn't seen her. She wasn't quite sure why she didn't want to meet him, for she loved him so much that she felt that she could never see enough of him, anyway. Possibly because the last time they had met he had called her a pretty little mouse. She turned her thoughts resolutely away from him and began a conversation with the student nurse who was helping her, a rather tiresome type who took pleasure in pointing out Becky's many faults on every occasion. She was being called to task quite severely because she had got her tenses mixed as usual, when Zuster Trippe stopped rather suddenly, letting the blanket fall. Becky swept her side tidily up the bed, mitred the corner neatly and said, her Dutch all wrong as usual: 'Why do you stop? You can't have finished grumbling at my mistakes . . .'

She was aware that the other girl was put out about something, indeed she had never seen her look so uncomfortable. The Directrice, thought Becky, who had a wholesome regard for that lady, and turned round smartly.

The Baron was in the doorway, watching silently, his registrar and houseman and the Hoofd Zuster peering round him, as though she and Zuster Trippe were putting on an exhibition of bedmaking for their benefit.

The Baron inclined his head politely. 'Zuster Saunders, I wish to speak to you.' He advanced into the ward. 'And I must compliment you on the improvement in your Dutch,' he gave Zuster Trippe a cold look as he spoke. 'I trust that you get all the help and encouragement you need.' He spoke softly to the Hoofd Zuster, who said something in her turn to everyone there, and Becky watched them all go away. She went a little pale; she had done something awful, although she couldn't think what—or perhaps Bertie was ill, or Pooch ... She raised troubled eyes to his face and said quickly: 'Oh, what have I done? Or is it the animals ...?'

The Baron seated himself on the side of a newly made-up bed. 'Why must you always imagine that I am the bearer of bad news?' he wanted to know with some asperity. 'That nurse was rather on the snappy side, wasn't she? What had you been doing?'

'Getting my grammar wrong—she fancies herself as a teacher, I think.'

'Your grammar is admittedly a little peculiar, but your accent is good,' and when she said eagerly: 'Oh, is it really? I am glad ...' he asked: 'Why are you so anxious to speak our language, Becky?'

She could hardly tell him that it was because she wanted to understand every word he uttered and even be able to answer him so that he would be able to understand her. 'Oh, I don't know,' she mumbled.

He hitched up his elegant trousers and stared at a shoe. 'My mother is to go to London in three days' time—I want her to see Mr Lennox ...' Becky knew of him; a famous orthopaedic surgeon whose opinion was sought all over the world. 'We're old friends,' went on the Baron. 'I want to make sure that everything is as good as it ever will be before she plunges back into her busy little life. She gardens, you know, not just a weed or two and picking flowers; she's quite capable of taking the spade from the gardener

and using it, and she has this thing about digging the
potato crop too. My father was able to manage her
in the nicest possible way, I'm not as successful—she
has done what she wants all her life, bless her, and it
would be cruel and impossible to stop her. All the
same, I'd like her looked at before she surprises us
with some new idea. Last year it was country danc-
ing . . .'

Becky smiled. 'It's nice to find someone who
doesn't moan about getting elderly. I don't think I've
ever met anyone who enjoyed life as she does.'

'You like her, Becky?'

'Yes, immensely.' She added silently: 'And I like
you too, Tiele, as well as loving you.'

'That's good. She has agreed to go to London, but
only if you will go with her. Tialda offered, but Pieter
isn't keen on her travelling around too much, and in
any case, my mother had already decided that she
wanted you to go.'

Becky folded a pillow case neatly. 'That's very nice
of her and I'd have loved to have gone, but I'm here,
aren't I?'

'Don't worry about that—I've already spoken to
the Directrice, she has no objection—it will only be
for three days.'

'Oh, but I can't leave Bertie and Pooch . . .'

He said patiently: 'Of course not. They can spend
the time at my home with Lola. Willem will look after
them—they know their way about there.'

'How do we go?'

'I shall drive, of course.' He sounded surprised at
her question. 'We can take the night ferry from the
Hoek.' He got up from the bed. 'Today's Friday;

Willem will collect you at eleven o'clock on Monday and bring you all out to Huize Raukema, we'll leave after lunch.' He sauntered to the door.

'Will I be staying at the hospital?' asked Becky.

'No. My mother will be examined on Tuesday afternoon, probably X-rayed then and possibly have a final check-up on the Wednesday. We shall return on the Thursday. You will of course accompany her to the hospital.'

He had gone before she could say anything else. He had said that she wouldn't be staying at the hospital; she supposed it would be an hotel, in which case would her wardrobe stand up to it? The vexed question kept her mind occupied while she finished off the beds, but after that she was too busy to think about it.

At lunch, as she was sitting with the other nurses of the ward, someone asked her what Doctor Raukema had wanted. 'He never talks to any of the nurses, though I suppose as you nursed his mother you know each other well.' There was faint envy in the voice.

'Well, no, not really,' said Becky, painstakingly truthful. 'His mother has to go to London to be examined and she wants me to go with her.'

There was a murmur of interest. 'And you go, naturally, Becky?'

'Doctor Raukema asked me if I would; it's only for a few days.'

'You are a lucky girl—will you have much free time?'

Becky remembered the Baroness's habit of forgetting things like off duty and whether she had had her lunch, and all the errands she wanted done. She smiled because despite that she was fond of the little lady. 'No, I don't expect I shall,' she admitted.

She decided against buying another dress; her slowly growing hoard of guldens was too precious and she doubted very much if she would wear it. She packed the green jersey dress, the flowered cotton skirt and the blouse that went with it and then recklessly went to C & A and bought a second one in very pale green with a ruffled collar and long sleeves ending in matching ruffles.

She was ready and waiting for Willem when he arrived. Mevrouw Botte, quite excited about the whole thing, toiled up the stairs to tell Becky he was there and then insisted on carrying her case down for her while Willem, who had come along at a more leisurely pace, took Bertie's lead, which left Becky, clutching Pooch, to go downstairs quite uncluttered. It gave her a lovely feeling, just as though she were beautiful and important, and somehow Willem contrived to go on making her feel like that in the car. He was driving a Porsche which he explained was used by the Baron occasionally, although he preferred the Rolls. 'And that's a very good car, Miss Saunders,' said Willem surprisingly, 'but for myself, I like something sporty.'

Becky digested this in silence; Willem hardly looked like a demon driver. Presently she asked: 'Doesn't the Baron like driving a fast car?'

They were already clear of Leeuwarden, racing along the road. 'Him drive fast? Why, I taught him to drive, Miss Saunders, when he was a lad. He's a great one for speed—you should just see him in that

Rolls of his when he's on his own.'

'You've known him a long time, haven't you, Willem?' She hoped they would go on talking about the Baron for a long time; it was lovely to find out about him, and Willem, she was delighted to discover, was nothing loath. The journey passed pleasantly for both of them. It was only a pity that they reached the gates of Huize Raukema before Willem had finished telling her about the Baron's more youthful days.

The master of the house wasn't home; Becky gathered from Sutske that he was seeing a patient, and the Baroness was expected shortly. With Bertie and Pooch ambling ahead of her, very much at home, she was led to the sitting room, its doors open to the garden beyond, and given coffee and a selection of the day's newspapers. She was painstakingly translating the small ads when the Baron arrived. The house was too large and solidly built for her to hear more than a murmur of voices, but she was quite sure who it was, for Bertie and Pooch were already hurrying to the door.

The Baron stopped to pull Bertie's ears, sweep Pooch up into an arm and warn Lola not to get excited and then came across the room to her with a brisk 'Good morning, Becky, everything is all right, I hope?' He sat down opposite her. 'I'm sorry I wasn't home when you arrived—a last-minute urgent case. Ah, here's Willem with more coffee. Be mother, will you, Becky?'

She poured the coffee from a tall silver pot into delicate white and lilac cups—early Delft and so old she was terrified of breaking something. She concentrated hard on what she was doing because she felt shy of him. Now if she had been beautiful and sure of herself like Nina van Doorn . . .

'What are you thinking about, Becky?' asked her companion. 'You look sad and excited all rolled into one. Is it a secret?'

She drew a breath. 'Yes.' And then, because she had to talk about something else and anyway she had been worrying away at something which had puzzled her for days: 'When we had that picnic—in the grounds of that dear little country house—whose was it?' And when he didn't answer at once: 'Was it yours, too?'

He passed his cup for more coffee and settled himself more comfortably. 'Yes, Becky, it is my house. And since you're so curious about it—I didn't want to tell you then—I had a feeling it might spoil the evening, you see. I . . .'

He didn't finish because the door was flung open and Nina came in. She looked lovelier than ever because she was in a towering rage. Beyond a furious look at Becky she didn't bother with her, but almost ran across the room to the Baron, who had got to his feet unhurriedly and was showing, Becky was relieved to see, no signs of alarm, nor was his calm shattered under the torrent of words Nina was pouring out. It was a pity that she spoke in Dutch, for Becky longed to know what she was so angry about. When she finally drew breath the Baron spoke—unhurriedly and as far as Becky could judge, good-humouredly, but Nina didn't like whatever he said. She raised her voice to an ugly shout and addressed Becky, who was none the wiser, added a rider to the

Baron and rushed out of the room.

'Well,' said Becky in an interested voice, 'what was all that about?'

'You,' said the Baron, and before she could get her mouth open to ask more, the door opened again and his mother came in.

In the bustle of getting the Baroness comfortably settled in a chair, pouring more coffee, retrieving the shawls, scarves and handbag which she had cast down on her way from the door to the sitting room, Becky had little time to ponder the Baron's reply. And when she did, sitting in the Rolls beside him while he drove them all down to the Hoek, she came to the conclusion that Nina had been upset because she wasn't a member of the party. It was a pity that no one had mentioned her. Lunch had been a pleasant meal with the Baroness bearing the lion's share of the conversation, and afterwards Becky had gone to the kitchen to bid Bertie and Pooch goodbye, and when she rejoined mother and son in the drawing room, the Baroness was talking about the weather. The Baron, for some reason, was looking amused.

They travelled in great comfort, but then Becky couldn't imagine the Baron doing anything else, and certainly not his mother, but it was pleasant, when they stopped briefly for tea, to have instant attention and smiling service. They stopped for dinner too, at Saur's in den Haag, and Becky thanked heaven silently that she was wearing the green jersey; it was hardly *haute couture* but it passed muster in a crowd, and the crowd was fashionable. Presumably the Baron had booked a table, for there was no delay for them, they had their drinks and were served at once;

iced soup followed by lobster and a salad because the Baron had recommended them and washed down by a dry white wine. And Becky was persuaded to sample a waffle smothered in whipped cream for desert and topped with strawberries before their coffee. She would have liked to have spent more time in den Haag. One day, she promised herself, she would go there on a day off and have a good look round.

They reached the Hoek shortly after, and here again there was no waiting about. The car was driven aboard, the Baroness made comfortable in her state-room, the steward warned as to what time they were to be wakened in the morning and by that time the ferry was already at sea. Becky, rather disappointed at the total absence of the Baron, went to the cabin next to the Baroness's and got ready for the night. The Baroness was already asleep when she crept in to see if she wanted anything; Becky left a dim light on, opened the door between them, and went to bed herself.

They breakfasted in their cabins and it was only as the ferry was docking that the Baron appeared, to wish them both good morning and swept them down into the car. True, he enquired as to whether they had had a good night, but he was so deep in thought that Becky kept a still tongue in her head and even suggested, once they were clear of Customs, that she should travel in the back with the Baroness—a suggestion nipped in the bud with a: 'What for?' from the Baron, uttered in a tone of voice which really didn't need an answer.

They were in London by mid-morning, and Becky,

who wasn't familiar with the city, watched idly from the window as they threaded their way through the traffic, but she couldn't help but see that they were passing through the most elegant streets and squares. When the Baron finally stopped in Carlos Place and she got out of the car, aided quite unnecessarily by a porter, she saw that they were outside the Connaught Hotel. She might not know her London well, but she had heard about some of its famous hotels. She thought with vexation of her inadequate wardrobe as she took the Baroness's arm and went into the splendid foyer. But only for a moment or so. After all, her clothes didn't really matter; she had come as companion to the Baroness and it wasn't likely that she would spend much time in its restaurant or public rooms. She watched the Baron getting things arranged without fuss and was wafted with her companion to the third floor, where a suite of rooms had been booked for them—a sitting room, an enormous bedroom for the Baroness with a smaller one for herself, bathrooms, and a room for the Baron. She still wasn't very happy about her clothes, but she unpacked for the Baroness and herself, assisted that lady to tidy herself and sat her down in the sitting room until the Baron should join them.

CHAPTER NINE

THEY had lunch in the hotel's restaurant and although Becky had suggested diffidently that mother and son might like to lunch alone while she had something in their sitting room, she had been met with such a blazing look from the Baron that she had stopped in mid-sentence. 'Do you not wish for our company?' he had asked her coldly, and when she had tried to explain, getting her lack of the right clothes hopelessly mixed up with the fact that she was only there as a companion anyway, and hadn't expected ... she had been cut short with such arrogance that she had remarked severely:

'Well, you have no need to be so nasty about it. I was trying to make it easier for you and the Baroness —after all I'm only ...'

'If you say that just once more,' said the Baron explosively, 'I shall do you an injury! Just because your stepmother and stepbrother treated you like a maid-of-all-work it doesn't mean to say that I, or my mother, intend to do the same. You will take your meals with us, Becky.'

She had been so taken aback by his arrogance that she had agreed meekly.

The arrogance had disappeared by the time they were shown to their table; the Baron was all smooth charm, putting her at ease with a skill only seconded by his parent. Becky found herself enjoying every moment—the excellent food, the rich surroundings, the waiter's attention. She began to sparkle just a little and when they had finished went off with the Baroness to assist that lady to make herself comfortable for an afternoon's rest. That done, she wandered into the sitting room and went to look out of the windows. London—the best part of London, flowed smoothly past her downbent gaze; she was so absorbed that she didn't hear the Baron come in until he joined her. She jumped nervously, intent as always on keeping a cool front towards him.

'Oh, I expect you want to sit here—I've heaps of things I can do in my room, I'll ...'

His hand came out and fastened gently on her arm. 'Becky, why do you always behave as though I'm an ogre?' He sighed. 'I've said some horrible things to you, haven't I? And now I discover that I didn't mean one of them.'

He smiled down at her and her heart rocked. She said stupidly: 'Oh, it doesn't matter,' and was inordinately vexed when he replied blandly: 'I know it doesn't.'

His hand tightened on her arm. 'Come and sit down while I tell you what has been arranged.' And when she was seated beside him: 'Mother will be seen by Mr Lennox tomorrow morning at ten o'clock. It will be your job to see that she is ready to leave here by half past nine, stay with her at all times while she is there and bring her back here. It is possible that he may wish to see her briefly in the afternoon; we shan't be leaving until the following evening, in any case. At half past three this afternoon I shall drive you both to the hospital where she will have her X-rays done. I'm afraid you will have to come back by taxi because I have an appointment at four-thirty and may not be ready in time to fetch you. I've already arranged for it to be waiting for you; the hall porter will see to that. I thought it might be pleasant to go to a theatre this evening—I've got tickets. We'll dine early—seven o'clock should be time enough.'

'Oh, but ...' began Becky, and then, completely reckless: 'That would be very nice, but have I time to go and buy a dress? I mean, I didn't expect to go out.'

He glanced at his watch. 'You have one hour exactly, take a taxi there and back.' He added reflectively: 'I was beginning to wonder just what you were saving your money for, Becky.'

She felt her cheeks redden. She could hardly say: 'To get away from you, my darling Tiele,' but instead she murmured something about having had no time and got to her feet. 'I promise I'll be back,' she told him breathlessly. 'Is it—will it be black tie, do you think?'

His mouth twitched just a little. 'Oh, yes—we're celebrating my mother's return to good health, are we not?'

From a visit years ago, Becky remembered that Fenwick's was in Bond Street, and that wasn't too far away. 'I'll go now,' she decided, and made for the door. The Baron had no difficulty in keeping up with her; he ushered her into the lift, escorted her to the pavement, told the doorman to get a taxi and handed her in. 'Where do you go?' he asked her.

'Well, Fenwick's, it's at the other end of Bond Street.'

He spoke to the driver, gave him some money, and put his head through the window. 'Buy something pretty,' he advised her, 'and I've settled with the man.'

Fenwick's didn't seem to have changed very much. Becky made her way to the gown department and set about the serious business of buying something pretty. It would have to be practical too, since it was an extravagance she didn't mean to repeat for a long time. She found what she wanted before long; a wide skirt in palest grey patterned with delicate pink roses and a pale pink crêpe blouse to wear with it. It cost more than she had bargained for, and she still had sandals to buy. Luckily there was quite a bit of the hour left; she hurried into Oxford Street and found exactly what she wanted—pale grey sandals with high heels. They were on the bargain rack outside the shop and although they looked like leather, they were plastic and very flimsy, but they would do. She almost ran into the street to find a taxi, terrified of being late.

At the hotel the doorman helped her out, assured her that he would pay the driver and called a boy to carry her parcels up to her room, where, with five minutes to spare, she had a quick look at the dress and hung it up before presenting herself in the sitting room.

'Ten minutes,' said the Baron. 'If you will start on my mother now.' He had been sitting by the window with his eyes shut, but now he got to his feet and wanted to know if she had had a successful time at the shops.

'Oh, yes, thank you,' said Becky happily, and went away to get the Baroness on to her feet.

At the hospital the Baron handed them over to a young man in a white coat who was introduced as Jimmy Mathers, before he excused himself and went back to the car, leaving Becky and the Baroness to be escorted to the X-ray department. The Baroness was inclined to be peevish and it took all Becky's tact to get her to do as she was asked. It was tedious, complained the little lady, having to come to the hospital—surely it could have been done at the hotel, and just when she wanted her tea ...

Becky promised tea, explained with patience why it was really better to attend the hospital and pointed out that the taxi was waiting for them the moment they were ready.

'Oh, well,' sighed the Baroness, 'let us get it over and done with, then.' She handed Becky her hand-bag and stick. 'You will come with me tomorrow, won't you, my dear?'

'Of course, Baroness. Now if you will just lie down here—I'll help you ...'

They were back at the hotel, half way through tea, when the Baron joined them. He refused tea, saying that he had already had it, and he stayed only a few minutes, explaining that he had to go out again. 'But don't forget that we are dining at seven o'clock,' he warned, as he went.

Becky dressed with care but no waste of time; the

Baroness had taken longer than usual, complaining that her legs ached, so that Becky had spent quite a while massaging them before helping her patient to dress. Now, wriggling into her outfit, she thanked heaven that her hair-style was a simple one and her make-up just as simple. The dress looked nice. She twirled to and fro before the wall mirror, looking closely at the sandals; at a distance and unless they were inspected very closely, they didn't look cheap at all. With a final pat to her already smooth hair, she went along to the sitting room. The Baroness would be waiting . . .

She wasn't, but the Baron was, standing with his back to the room, looking out of one of the windows. Her heart danced at the sight of his broad shoulders, elegant in his black jacket, and it danced even harder when he turned round.

'I always thought you were nice to look at,' he told her softly. 'You look very pretty, Becky—indeed, I might say beautiful.'

She paused in the doorway feeling shy and happy and sad all rolled into one.

'Thank you, but it's not true, you know. I mean, when you think of Juffrouw van Doorn . . .'

'But I'm not thinking of her.'

Her eyes were very dark. 'Yes—well, I think you should be. I mean . . .'

'Just what do you mean, Becky?'

She was pleating a fold of her skirt in nervous fingers, wishing she had never started this conversation. 'She's so beautiful,' she managed at last.

'Do you know what I told her that day she came—

you remember? just before we left home?' He strolled across the room to stand before her, staring down into her upturned face.

She thought how very blue his eyes were. 'No.'

'I told her that I was going to marry you.' He stooped and kissed her. 'No, don't say a word; you're going to tell me that you don't believe it, and I'm not surprised, I didn't believe it myself at first. Just get used to the idea, Becky.'

She had no words and no breath, and perhaps it was just as well that the Baroness came into the room at that moment, demanding with charming persistence that someone should give her a drink. Becky was given a glass too and drank its contents, not having the least notion what it was. She had no idea what she ate at dinner either; she sat in a dreamlike state answering when she was spoken to, avoiding Tiele's eye, prudently refusing more than one glass of the champagne he had ordered; she was muddled enough as it was.

She became even more muddled as the evening wore on. Nothing in the Baron's manner bore out his astonishing remarks to her before dinner; he treated her with a placid friendliness which made her wonder if she had dreamed the whole thing—only, she told herself, no one could dream up a kiss like the one he had given her. She sat between mother and son, her eyes on the stage, seeing nothing of the play, and feeling so peculiar that she began to wonder if it was the champagne. But it wasn't the champagne, she knew that when Tiele possessed himself of her hand, holding it gently in a cool, firm grip.

But he said nothing. They went back to the hotel

when the play was over and had a light supper in the restaurant and presently the Baroness said that she really would have to go to bed and Becky, terrified of being left alone with Tiele although it was the one thing she most wanted to happen, accompanied her to her room and helped her to her bed. Tiele had bidden them both goodnight, and if Becky had hoped secretly that he would suggest that she should join him again, she took care not to admit it, even to herself.

He had gone out when she went along to the sitting room in the morning. She made a quick breakfast and then spent the next hour making sure that the Baroness would be ready to leave at half past nine—something which was achieved, but only just. The Baron returned punctually, wished them a cheerful good morning and without waste of time drove them to the hospital. Becky, studying him covertly, could see no signs of a man in love, especially with herself. He handed them over to the care of the Orthopaedic Ward Sister, observed that he would see them later, and went away.

Mr Lennox was a thorough man. The Baroness, examined exhaustively, was allowed to leave about noon with the request that she should return that afternoon. 'A final test or two,' said Mr Lennox soothingly. 'Let your nurse bring you back at three o'clock. There will be no need for her to wait, I shall have the pleasure of driving you back to your hotel myself.'

There was no sign of the Baron when they got back to the hotel. They lunched in the sitting room, discussing the morning's activities, and after the Baroness

had rested Becky called a taxi and took her back to
the hospital, prudently leaving a note for the Baron.

It was well after three o'clock by the time Becky
had satisfied herself that the Baroness was in good
hands and that Mr Lennox really did intend to take
her back later. 'Go and enjoy yourself, my dear,'
begged the Baroness. 'They tell me that I shan't be
leaving here for an hour—why not do some shopping? If I'm not back by five o'clock, you can telephone . . .'

Becky bade her a cheerful goodbye. She wasn't going to do any shopping; she was going to get on a bus
and go to the nearest park and walk, perhaps that
would clear her head. She went briskly through the
entrance, across the forecourt and on to the crowded
pavement—right into the arms of Basil.

The shock sent the colour from her cheeks and
rendered her dumb. She could only stand and stare at
him, grinning down at her with a look of vindictive
triumph. It was only when he put a hand on her arm
that she tried to wrench it away and couldn't.

'Not so fast, Rebecca.' Basil's voice was as smooth
and nasty as it had always been. 'What a gift from
heaven, my dear, dear Rebecca! Mother isn't really
up to running the house, you know, and somehow
the housekeepers we engage don't stay more than a
week or two. She'll be delighted to see you again—
you shall come back with me . . .'

'I won't!' said Becky fiercely. 'And you can't make
me. I've a good job and I'd rather die than go back.'

'At the hospital, are you? Well, it shouldn't be too
hard to cook up some reason why you should come
home, but it would be far better for you, little step-

sister, if you came quietly with me now.'

She gave another tug and his grip tightened. She didn't like the idea of making a scene, it would mean the police, probably, and that would involve the Baroness and Tiele. At the thought of him she said desperately: 'Oh, Tiele!'

The Baron, standing on the other side of the street watching, frowned. He had been on the point of going into the hospital, waiting for the traffic to allow him to cross. Now he didn't wait, but dodged between buses and taxis and cars and gained the pavement in time to hear Basil say: 'Don't be a fool, Rebecca! You can't make a scene here—come along ...'

The Baron's voice, very soft, sent Becky's heart soaring. 'Not so fast, my friend. Rebecca stays where she is.' He added in a voice which sent shivers down her back: 'You are the unspeakable Basil, I take it?'

Basil went a rich plum colour. 'And who are you?' he blustered. 'What right have you to interfere?'

'All the right in the world, my good fellow; Rebecca is going to be my wife.' His hand closed like a vice on Basil's arm and plucked it away from Becky. 'You mentioned making a scene—I have no inhibitions about doing so; if you are not out of my sight in ten seconds, I'll make a scene you will never forget.'

It was amazing how very quickly Basil melted into the unnoticing passers-by. Becky, very pale still, stood shivering, and Tiele slid a vast arm round her shoulders.

'A nice cup of tea,' he observed placidly, 'is just what we need.' But when Becky looked at his face, his eyes weren't placid at all, they were dark blue with rage.

She said apologetically: 'I'm sorry—he took me by surprise, and I was frightened. I'm all right now ...'

'Are you indeed? The colour of watered milk and shaking like a fairy in a snowstorm.'

'You're angry.'

His smile warmed her. 'Yes, but that cup of tea will soothe me back to my usual arrogant, ill-mannered self.'

She closed her eyes for a moment. 'Don't say that —it's not true.' She opened them to tell him: 'I called you and you came.'

'Let us say rather that kindly providence arranged for me to be on my way to meet you at the hospital— I was on the other side of the street.' He took his arm from her shoulders and put a hand under her arm. 'There's an Olde-Worlde Tea Shoppe in the next street—it's rather out of its environment and it's run by a dragon with a light hand at pastry.'

Becky, who had been wanting to cry, giggled instead. 'I don't suppose you know the first thing about pastry.'

He walked her down a narrow turning, round a corner and into a quiet little cul-de-sac, unexpected and almost rural in the centre of the city. The tea room was at its end, sandwiched between a narrow house with window boxes and a tiny dress shop called 'Angel's Boutique'. There weren't many people sitting at the small round tables, and the Baron chose one at a window, so that he could sit on the window seat. 'For I doubt if these chairs are up to my weight,' he explained, and then turned to smile with tremendous charm at the light-handed dragon, already hovering.

'Tea, if you please,' he begged her in a voice as charming as his smile, 'and some of your little cakes —and perhaps a plate of thinly cut bread and butter.'

'Tea is not tea without bread and butter,' observed the dragon severely. 'I am glad that there are some people who know what is right and proper.' She sent a chilling glance at the two girls sitting close by, with a dish of éclairs between them and no bread and butter in sight. When she had gone Tiele remarked: 'I'll wager my table silver that she's been someone's nanny.'

Becky was feeling better. 'The bread and butter bit? Yes, I think you're right. Tiele, do you think he'll come back for me?—Basil?'

He stretched a hand across the table and took hers in its secure grasp. 'No, my darling, he won't come back again, and I shall be there if he does.'

'Oh, why do you ...' She broke off as the dragon arrived with a tray and arranged everything just so before leaving them again.

Just as though she had finished the sentence he answered her: 'You are my darling. Becky, it took me a little while to discover it—and to admit it—but now I find that I cannot live without you, nor do I wish to.'

He poured the tea for them both and passed her a cup. 'Drink that, my dearest heart—you've had a bad fright.' He hadn't let go of her hand and she took no notice of the tea, only sat there staring at him.

'Nina?' she spoke under her breath.

'She loved my money, Becky darling, not me.'

Becky heaved a deep sigh. 'I love you,' she said simply. 'But didn't you l-love her at all?'

He shook his head. 'No. I took her out a good deal; she amused me ... But I don't want to be amused in that way, darling—Oh, I shall laugh at you a dozen times a day, but we shall share our laughter.'

He was interrupted by the dragon who swept up to the table, wanting to know if the bread and butter wasn't to their liking. 'Because you've eaten none of it,' she pointed out severely.

Tiele charmed her with another smile. 'It is quite perfect,' he told her. 'We are about to eat every morsel.'

She smiled then, looking at them in turn. 'Well, you don't have to hurry,' she said as she went away.

Becky was made to eat her tea then and when she tried to get her hand back Tiele engulfed it even more tightly. 'No, you'll have to manage with the other one,' he told her. 'I've been wanting to hold your hand for a long time, and now that I have it, I don't intend to let it go.'

Becky obediently ate her bread and butter. Half way through the second slice she said: 'It doesn't seem true ... I can't believe ... Tiele, I'm plain and I haven't any pretty clothes and I'm not witty—and your big house terrifies me even though I love it.'

He lifted her hand and kissed it gently. 'You're the most beautiful girl in the world and I'm going to give you all the pretty clothes you could possibly want. I don't like witty girls with shrill voices—you have a lovely voice, my darling.' He grinned at her. 'And when the house has some children in it, it won't seem so large.'

He poured more tea and Becky, suddenly on top of her world, took one of the cakes he was offering her. She said a little shyly: 'People in love aren't supposed to eat . . .'

'Then we will be the exception to the rule, my love.'

Presently they bade the dragon goodbye and wandered out into the street. There was no one about, only the dragon watching them through a window.

'We must go back,' said Becky. 'Your mother will wonder what has happened.'

'No, she won't—she knows that I'm going to marry you.'

'Are you?' asked Becky demurely. 'I haven't been asked yet.'

The words were no sooner out of her mouth before she was in his arms.

'Dare to say no,' said the Baron, and gave her no chance to say anything at all. Being kissed like that, thought Becky hazily, took all one's breath; to try to speak would be a waste of time. She kissed him back instead, and the dragon, looking fiercer than ever, wiped away a sentimental tear and nodded her head with satisfaction.

Harlequin Presents...

The beauty of true romance...

The excitement of world travel...

The splendor of first love...

Remember when a good love story made you feel like holding hands?

The wonder of love is timeless. Once discovered, love remains, despite the passage of time. Harlequin brings you stories of true love, about women the world over—women like you.

Harlequin Romances with the Harlequin magic...

Recapture the sparkle of first love...relive the joy of true romance...enjoy these stories of love today.

Six new novels every month— wherever paperbacks are sold.

What the press says about Harlequin Romances...

"...clean, wholesome fiction...always with an upbeat, happy ending."
—*San Francisco Chronicle*

"...a work of art."
—*The Globe & Mail*, Toronto

"Nothing quite like it has happened since *Gone With the Wind...*"
—*Los Angeles Times*

"...among the top ten..."
—*International Herald-Tribune*, Paris

"The most popular reading matter of American women today."
— *The Detroit News*

"Women have come to trust these clean easy-to-read stories about contemporary people, set in exciting foreign places."
— *Best Sellers*, New York

"Harlequin novels have a vast and loyal readership."
— *Toronto Star*

NEW FROM HARLEQUIN

YOUR 1980 ROMANCE HOROSCOPE!

Harlequin Reader Service

In U.S.A.
M.P.O. Box 707
Niagara Falls, NY 14302

In Canada
649 Ontario Street
Stratford, Ontario, N5A 6W2

Please send me the following Harlequin Romance Horoscope volumes. I am enclosing a check or money order of $1.75 for each volume ordered, plus 40¢ to cover postage and handling.

☐ **Aries**
(Mar 21-Apr 20)

☐ **Taurus**
(Apr 21-May 22)

☐ **Gemini**
(May 23-June 21)

☐ **Cancer**
(June 22-July 22)

☐ **Leo**
(July 23-Aug. 22)

☐ **Virgo**
(Aug. 23-Sept. 22)

☐ **Libra**
(Sept. 23-Oct. 22)

☐ **Scorpio**
(Oct. 23-Nov. 21)

☐ **Sagittarius**
(Nov. 22-Dec. 22)

☐ **Capricorn**
(Dec. 23-Jan. 20)

☐ **Aquarius**
(Jan. 21-Feb. 19)

☐ **Pisces**
(Feb. 20-Mar 20)

Number of volumes checked @ $1.75 each $_____

N.Y. and N.J. residents add appropriate sales tax $_____

Postage and handling $_____ .40

                                              TOTAL: $_____

I am enclosing a grand total of $_____

NAME_____

ADDRESS_____

STATE/PROV._____ ZIP/POSTAL CODE_____

ROM 2301